'You've been missed, my dear Babs.'

Her pulses raced; she hardly dared look at him. What did he mean — that he missed her on duty, or personally, emotionally, physically? Babs met his eyes. She felt as if she were melting under his gaze. It seemed deathly quiet in the office. She put a hand on the desk to steady herself, and said, her voice seeming to come from a long way off, pleading, 'No, Guy, you mustn't look at me like that.'

Dear Reader

We continue with our quartet, LONG HOT SUMMER, in which Babs starts work in the rehabilitation unit, and complete the Lennox duet with LEGACY OF SHADOWS, where Christy has to face her past. Jenny Ashe takes us to Singapore, an area she knows well, in IN THE HEAT OF THE SUN, and from Caroline Anderson we have PICKING UP THE PIECES. Nick, in her previous book SECOND THOUGHTS, demanded his own story, and this is it. Just what you need in cold February to warm you. Enjoy!

The Editor

Margaret O'Neill started scribbling at four and began nursing at twenty. She contracted TB, and, when recovered, did her British Tuberculosis Association nursing training before general training at the Royal Portsmouth Hospital. She married, had two children, and, with her late husband, she owned and managed several nursing homes. Now retired and living in Sussex, she still has many nursing contacts. Her husband would have been delighted to see her books in print.

Recent titles by the same author:

NEVER PAST LOVING
CHRISTMAS IS FOREVER

LONG HOT SUMMER

BY

MARGARET O'NEILL

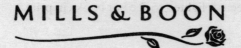

MILLS & BOON

MILLS & BOON LIMITED
ETON HOUSE, 18–24 PARADISE ROAD
RICHMOND, SURREY, TW9 1SR

First published in Great Britain 1993
by Mills & Boon Limited

© Margaret O'Neill 1993

Australian copyright 1993
Philippine copyright 1994
This edition 1994

ISBN 0 263 78475 4

Set in 10 on 12 pt Linotron Times
03-9402-50747

Typeset in Great Britain by Centracet, Cambridge
Made and printed in Great Britain

CHAPTER ONE

THE sun blazed down out of a cloudless blue sky and the air beneath the canopy at Park station was motionless as Babs alighted from the train. Not a breath of air stirred the hem of her thin cotton skirt.

She asked at the ticket barrier, 'Do you think there'll be a taxi along soon?'

'No idea,' replied the ticket collector. 'Where d'ya want to get to?'

'Princes Park Hospital.'

'You a student, then?'

'No, I'm a nurse, a staff nurse.'

''Struth, they get younger every day.'

'I've heard that before.'

'And prettier. But I suppose you've heard that before too.'

Babs smiled and nodded. In spite of being tired and thirsty, she was enjoying the conversation. She was a friendly girl, uninhibited and interested in other people, which was what made her, at twenty-two, a splendid nurse with a great future before her.

'Since this benighted station doesn't run to a refreshment bar,' she teased, 'is there anywhere near by where I can get something to drink?'

'There's Rosie's Caff over the level crossing, and you might be lucky if you go there, and get a lift to the hospital; there's often someone from the hospital there.

And if you're not in luck, I'll get the next taxi bloke who comes in to pick you up. OK?'

'Couldn't be better, thanks very much.' She gave the man a dazzling smile as she bent to collect her bags and cases.

He grinned in return. 'Go on, you can leave your luggage with me if y'like. I'll keep an eye on it.'

'You are kind.'

'Hmmph.'

Babs made her way over the railway lines that shimmered in the fierce sunshine as they curved away between the hills and trees of the Surrey-Hampshire borders, throbbing in the late afternoon heat.

The café was empty. The middle-aged lady behind the counter—Rosie, presumably—looked as hot and tired as Babs herself, but she conjured up a smile of sorts when Babs ordered tea.

'Would you like iced lemon or ordinary?'

'Iced lemon sounds nice and refreshing.'

'Going up to the hospital?' asked Rosie as she poured the tea into a tall glass, and then, pointing to the covered shelf, continued, 'Bun or something?'

'Yes to both.' Babs smiled. 'I'll be a devil and have two buns, please, and to hell with my diet.'

Rosie looked her slender, boyish figure up and down. 'I bet you don't have to do any damned silly dieting.' She sighed. 'Not like me; I'm forever trying the latest "get slim fast" diet, but what happens? A week after I finish, the pounds are going on faster than they came off.'

Babs took a sip of tea, followed by a mouthful of

bun. She smiled sympathetically at the plump lady. 'I'm lucky,' she said. 'I burn up everything fast.'

'I'd give anything to do that,' said Rosie wistfully. 'You'd never believe that I'm on my feet all day, and never touch any of these.' She waved her hand over the counter, laden with cakes and pastries. 'It just ain't fair.' She grinned.

Babs agreed, and at that moment the doorbell clanged as somebody came into the café.

'Well, you're in luck,' said Rosie. 'This is a doctor — well, a surgeon — up at Princes.' She turned to address the man standing in the doorway. 'Are you going up to the hospital, Mr Mansfield? Because if you are, this young lady would like a lift.'

Babs, for all her usual self-confidence, wished that Rosie hadn't been quite so blunt with her request. The man standing in the doorway was obviously a senior member of staff. He was grey-haired, and handsome in a thin, sombre sort of way, but without any sparkle. Not the sort of man to ask favours of, Babs thought.

'Oh, right,' he said without particular enthusiasm. He nodded to Babs. 'I'll give you a lift after I've had a cup of iced tea. That is if you don't mind waiting?' he asked, in a tone of voice that suggested that he didn't really care whether she minded or not.

'Of course not,' she said. 'I'm grateful to you. Anyway, I haven't finished my tea yet, or Rosie's delicious bun.'

Mr Mansfield seemed to eye the bun with distaste.

'All that cholesterol,' he said. 'Not to mention what it's doing to your teeth.'

Babs shrugged. 'I like living dangerously,' she said

with a smile. 'Besides, if one gets enough exercise and scrubs one's teeth ——'

'Forget it.' He seemed to have lost interest in the argument. 'Now do you mind telling me who you are? A patient?' His pale eyes looked her over. 'No, not unless you are a very fit one going for a check-up. New member of staff, perhaps?'

'Got it in two,' replied Babs, with a laugh. She had lost her initial feeling of inferiority with the surgeon, who, she realised, was not very old; he'd obviously just gone grey at an early age. It was his stuffy manner that made him seem older. 'I'm the new staff nurse,' she explained, 'on the rehabilitation unit, which, as you must know, is also pretty new.'

His lips set in a grim line. 'Yes, indeed, captured everyone's imagination and got high funding for the project. Lot of other causes the money could have gone to, but it beat the lot.'

'But surely every department benefits from Rehabilitation?'

'Yes, but to a minor degree; the money could have been better distributed.' He shrugged. 'As it is, no expense has been spared to install all the latest gadgetry.'

'Surely as a surgeon you welcome rehab work, whatever your field. It's obvious of course for bone and joint recovery, but every patient benefits post-operatively, don't you agree?'

'To a degree,' he conceded reluctantly.

'Then it proves my point,' said Babs. 'Every department of the hospital will benefit from the new rehabilitation centre.'

Mr Mansfield nodded. 'Probably,' he said abruptly. 'Now, Miss—er. . . I don't know your name.'

'It's not a state secret,' said Babs cheerfully, ignoring his abrasive attitude. She held out her hand. 'I'm Barbara Becker-Brown,' she said, 'Babs to my friends.'

'Roger Mansfield,' said her companion. 'Senior registrar. Cardio-thoracic unit.'

'So I'll be seeing some of your long-term patients from time to time,' Babs said, grinning broadly.

'Highly likely,' confirmed Mr Mansfield shortly.

Ten minutes later, having collected her baggage from the friendly ticket collector, they were on their way to Princes Park, and making rather dull conversation.

'Did you come here for your interview?' asked Mr Mansfield as they started up the long, winding drive to the hospital.

'No. I was nursing in Scotland, and had my interview in Edinburgh.'

'Did you like Scotland?'

'Loved it, would have stayed if I'd been offered rehabilitation work up there.'

'You're committed to rehabilitation?'

'Yes, now that more patients, young and old, are being given the chance to survive all manner of illnesses and accidents, I feel that it is the most constructive part of medicine. With rehabilitation, people don't just survive, they enjoy living. Their quality of life is enhanced immeasurably.'

'You're a convert,' said the surgeon, sounding sarcastic. 'The most dangerous kind of devotee.'

Babs said forcefully, 'Dangerous because I believe

that the extent to which a patient can be helped often goes beyond normal convalescence? Yes, I would agree with that.'

They slowed to go round a sharp bend between fir trees. The road widened out and was lined by rhododendrons in full bloom, their beauty marred by a thin coating of dust stirred up from the hot, dry surface of the driveway.

They rounded another bend, and there, sitting on the grass verge, was a bronzed, blond, virile-looking man in a singlet and brief shorts. He signalled for them to stop.

Mr Mansfield groaned and began slowing down.

'Do you know who it is?' asked Babs, staring with admiration at the man lounging on the grass.

'I do indeed,' said the doctor. 'It's Guy Lloyd. You'll be seeing plenty of him; he's the registrar on your precious rehabilitation unit, and a real fitness fanatic. I wonder what he's done this time.'

They stopped beside the reclining figure.

'Hi, Roger,' Guy said cheerfully. He raised a hand in salute and smiled. Babs blinked as she caught the full force of his smile and was subjected to a rapid inspection by a pair of the bluest eyes she had ever seen. They were a brilliant, blazing blue against a deeply tanned face, topped by a cap of blond-white hair. 'And who,' he said, his eyes lingering on Babs's face, his voice dropping a notch, 'may I ask, is the lady?' His voice was as deep and smooth as his tan.

'Barbara Becker-Brown, new staff nurse on your unit,' said Roger in a flat voice. 'And she knows who you are, Lloyd.'

'Do you?' asked Guy Lloyd, his fabulous blue eyes twinkling. 'Either my fame has travelled far, or Roger has been telling tales out of school, right?'

'The latter,' said Babs, smiling back at him, and trying to ignore the peculiar sensation that those brilliant blue eyes were having on her.

'You must think me all kinds of an idiot.' It was half a question, half a statement.

'I haven't heard anything to confirm that,' she said with a laugh. 'Just enough to make it sound as if you lead an adventurous sort of life.' She exchanged another smile with her registrar.

'Dear old Roger here thinks that I am accident-prone, but I'm not, you know. I try to break new ground, exercise-wise, and sometimes come the occasional cropper.'

'Sounds reasonable,' said Babs, telling herself that it was the heat that made her feel peculiarly breathless when her eyes met Guy's.

'It's not as reasonable as it might seem,' said Roger irritably. 'What you don't know is that Guy's recently had a chest infection, which didn't respond to the usual treatment. He's only just on the mend, working half-time, and is supposed to be taking things easy.'

Guy held up a warning hand. 'For goodness' sake, Roger, dry up. The poor girl doesn't want to hear all that rubbish about me; anyone would think that I was half dead, the way you tell it. It may surprise you, but I was taking it easy, just gently jogging.'

'Rehabilitating,' said Babs with a laugh. 'Are you allowed to run?'

'Of course, down the drive and back at a slow jog. I

only stopped because I've twisted my ankle, nothing to do with my chest.'

Roger crouched down and examined Guy's ankle without removing his running shoes and socks. 'Won't touch it till we get you up to Casualty,' he said. 'Probably a sprain needing a cold compress and support bandage, but we won't take any chances; they'll do a couple of X-rays to make sure that it's nothing worse.'

'Stop fussing, Roger, you're making a mountain out of a molehill. I'd trust you with my heart any time, but a simple twisted ankle? No way! Let Barbara, our new staff nurse, take a look and give an opinion.' Guy shot a conspiratorial smile at Babs, which, to her fury, made her feel most odd.

'Not Barbara—Babs,' she said. 'But I don't think that I should. . .' She looked helplessly at the two men, for once at a loss. She was cross with Guy Lloyd for putting her on the spot. How could she, a humble staff nurse, and new at that, contradict a senior registrar? Her feelings must have shown in her face, for Guy reached up and patted her hand.

'Sorry, stupid suggestion,' he said. 'Forget it.' He turned to Roger. 'I'm all yours, old chap,' he said cheerfully. 'Let's get this show on the road.'

Roger simply nodded, and together he and Babs helped Guy into the rear seat of the car, with his injured foot elevated into the most comfortable position. He drove slowly up the rest of the long drive, easing the car over the speed bumps that occurred at regular intervals, obviously to avoid jolting Guy's foot.

As the elegant façade of the main hospital building

came into sight, he asked Babs, 'Have you to report to Matron or the nurses' home manager first?'

'The home manager; she's going to show me my room and so on. And I hope I'll have time to shower and change before seeing Matron. I feel hot and sticky after all that travelling.' She ran a hand through her short tawny hair.

Guy grinned. 'That's right, must put on your best bib and tucker for our gorgon of a matron,' he teased. 'Make a good first impression and life may just be bearable.'

Roger stopped outside a building which was obviously the nurses' home. It was modern, but great care had been taken to make sure that it blended well with the older, gracious administration building that was the heart of Princes Park.

He began unloading her baggage before Babs was out of her seat. 'I'll put these inside the door,' he said, picking up all but one bag.

Babs ran after him. 'Really, there's no need, Mr Mansfield,' she said. 'I can manage.'

'It's no trouble,' he said dismissively.

'Well, thank you.' She followed him towards the building, but looked back at the car.

Guy was looking out of the open rear window. Even from this distance Babs felt the magnetism of his blazing blue eyes. She raised a hand. 'Goodbye,' she called softly. 'Hope your ankle's all right.'

'Thanks. Good luck; see you around.'

Roger Mansfield piled Babs's luggage in the hall beside a door marked 'Home Manager'. 'Miss Hannay will look after you,' he said. He strode back to the exit, cutting short her words of thanks as he left.

She watched him disappear through the front door with the feeling that now he and Guy had gone she was truly on her own, about to face her first official encounter — if one discounted her interview in far-off Edinburgh — with Princes Park authority.

She breathed in hard, and knocked at the home manager's door.

Two hours later, having weathered her meeting with the motherly home manager Marjory Hannay, and the elegant but, so she had been assured, kindly matron, Clare Dunn, Babs found herself in the staff club-room.

It had been Matron's idea that she visit the club. Her dark blue eyes had twinkled as she made the suggestion.

'It'll help you unwind after your long journey, and the dreaded interview with this gorgon of a matron,' she had said with a laugh. It was almost as if she had overheard Guy Lloyd's facetious description of her, but she had dispelled this idea by saying, 'It's all right, Nurse, it's just the traditional label for any matron over fifty, and I'm rather more than that.'

Babs was amused by Matron's sense of humour. She had dreaded the interview, though the administrative sister who had seen her in Edinburgh had assured her that Matron Dunn was rather special, and much loved by her staff. After meeting her, Babs could understand why she was regarded with such affection.

Matron herself had escorted Babs to the club-room, where she handed her over to a nurse who was just about to enter the building. 'Nurse Long will look after you, my dear, won't you, Gemma?' she asked the nurse, who had obviously just come off duty, and had removed her cap from a mass of flaming red hair tumbling round her shoulders.

'Sure, Matron,' replied the nurse with a faintly Irish accent.

'Thank you, Staff; let me introduce Barbara Becker-Brown, the new staff nurse on the rehab unit. She likes to be known as Babs.'

'Well, that's a blessing,' said Gemma. 'Your full title's quite a mouthful.' She held out a hand. 'Welcome to Princes, Babs. Sure, and you're going to love it here. It's a great place to work, and even our matron's not too bad,' she finished, pretending that Miss Dunn wasn't there.

'In my office at nine sharp tomorrow morning, Nurse, for disciplinary action,' said Matron, smiling broadly. 'On a charge of gross insubordination.'

'Yes, ma'am,' said Gemma, sketching a salute of sorts.

Matron turned to Babs. 'Well, goodnight, my dear, and good luck tomorrow when you start work. I'll see you on my rounds.' She smiled at both girls and walked back along the path towards the gracious Edwardian building and her office.

'She's an absolute cracker of a matron,' said Gemma softly, her accent more marked. 'An absolute cracker.' She took Babs's arm. 'Now come in and meet the rest of the family,' she said cheerfully, and together they entered the noisy club-room.

* * *

Later that night, settling down in her pretty bedroom, Babs reviewed her day and thought of the people she had met since arriving at Princes Park.

She thought especially of Guy Lloyd, so handsome with his short blond hair, tanned features and wickedly blue eyes, which had sent her pulses racing. He would be fun to work and play with, she guessed, but she had the feeling that he wasn't as casual as he first seemed. Beneath that sunny façade there was steel, and he had about him an air of serious authority and dedication. She had sensed it even when he was crouched at the side of the drive; he had seemed confident, sure of himself. She imagined that he would be a stickler to work with, which suited her fine, for with her work definitely came first and fun second.

She made a conscious effort to forget the sensation that his blue eyes had caused, and fell quickly into a happy and dreamless sleep.

CHAPTER TWO

BABS knew from the moment she started working in the rehab unit that she was going to love it. Just one thing gave her a stab of disappointment, and that was the absence of Guy Lloyd. She had looked forward to seeing him again, after their meeting on the drive the previous afternoon. She had felt then a desire to know the man better, and the desire persisted, although she tried to squash it as being ridiculous after a first meeting. But there was something intriguing about him, something that went deeper than superficial attractiveness. Those blue eyes and casually cheerful manner concealed a mature and sophisticated man.

She learned that he was not in the unit constantly, as he was partly engaged elsewhere in the hospital. He was attached to the unit in a special capacity as registrar, on account of the twenty cubicled rooms on the block, where some long-term patients resided prior to discharge. It was because of this new concept in rehabilitation care that both a registrar and nursing staff had been appointed.

He was frequently in and out of the unit, but Babs had missed him, and it was not until the third day after she had started work that he appeared while she was on duty.

It was late morning, and she was waist-deep in the hydrotherapy pool, helping physio teach a large young

paraplegic a few simple swimming strokes, when she
saw Guy enter the pool area, and a little prickle of
excitement went through her. The patient was scared,
and both Babs and Jane White were working hard to
reassure him.

'You're quite safe, Colin,' Babs was saying for the
umpteenth time, 'what with your floaters and Jane and
I standing by. Just let go of the rail for a minute and
try moving your arms. They're very strong; it's only
your legs that won't work properly.'

'I know that,' said Colin, fear making him irritable.
'But it's just that I never learned to swim. I don't like
swimming.'

'Can I help?' called Guy, white coat flapping as he
limped, with the aid of a stick, along the matt cork
non-slip surround of the pool. 'I've been given a clean
bill of health chest-wise.' He thumped his chest with a
Tarzan-like gesture. 'And I've got to swim to help my
ankle.'

Clearly Jane was pleased to see him. She waved, and
called out facetiously, 'Are you coming in as a patient,
or as our registrar, Doctor?'

'Both,' Guy replied. He laid his stick on the side-
bench and stripped off his white coat, trousers and T-
shirt, revealing a pair of brief black swimming-trunks.
He looked stunning, with his bleached blond cap of
hair, his dark golden tan and athletic physique. Like
an advertisement for a health and fitness magazine.
Babs swallowed an exclamation of admiration, and
bent her head to hide her reaction.

'Cor,' exclaimed Colin. 'He looks brilliant.' His voice
sank almost to a whisper. 'It isn't fair,' he said in a

wobbly voice, 'looking like that, and look at me. . .' He pointed to his helpless legs, supported by the water. 'Useless.'

Jane, her face gentle with compassion, said, 'You can. . .will improve as time goes on, Colin.' She looked helplessly at Babs.

Babs said, almost roughly, 'Life isn't fair, Colin, so it's no good beefing about it. Just get on with what you can do to help yourself. In the water you're not much different from Dr Lloyd. You're a nice-looking chap; make the most of it.'

For one interminable moment she thought that she had gone too far and that Colin would either burst into tears or lash out at her. Of the two, she would prefer the latter; at least it would show that he'd plenty of fight left in him, and fight was what he needed in his condition. Jane gasped, and looked horrified at her bluntness.

Colin stared at Babs, his young face a mixture of emotions, then suddenly he smiled and his smile changed to a laugh. 'Well, you certainly don't pull your punches, Nurse, do you?' he said cheerfully. He took his hand from the support rail and gave Babs a playful push. 'Watch this, then.' He took his other hand from the rail and tried a few tentative strokes, while Jane kept one hand under his chin and the other under his chest.

Guy had slipped into the water on the other side of the pool while this little pantomime was being enacted; now he joined them with a few easy strokes, dog-paddling to stay beside them and give encouragement

as Colin worked hard with his arms to pull himself
along.

After a while, Guy called a halt. 'That's it; you've
done enough for today, old chap, considering that this
time last week we couldn't even persuade you into the
pool. You've done wonders this morning. I'm proud of
you.'

'You can thank Nurse Bossy Boots here,' said Colin,
splashing water at Babs. 'She gave me a right ticking
off, I can tell you.'

'Well, it worked; that's the main thing.' Guy smiled
at all three of them and then said to Babs, 'Good
effort; we've been trying to get Colin moving for some
time. I knew you were going to be an asset to the
department when I met you the other afternoon. Well
done, and thanks.' He saluted them all and sped off
through the water with long, easy strokes, his wide
shoulders glistening with drops of water as he powered
himself along.

Babs felt herself blushing with pleasure at the compliment he'd paid her about her work. For one mad
moment, watching him move gracefully through the
water, she wondered what it would be like to be held
by his strong arms, and feel his bronzed body pressed
close to hers. . . Colin was speaking; she pulled herself
together with a jerk.

'One day,' said Colin, staring after him, 'I'm going
to challenge Doc to a race. What do you think my
chances of winning will be, Jane?'

Both he and Babs looked at Jane expectantly, and
Babs was surprised to find that Jane was looking at her

in a most unfriendly fashion, her usually kind eyes hard with dislike.

'Jane, is anything wrong?' she asked.

'Of course nothing's wrong,' said Jane sharply, producing a tight smile. 'And I think, Colin, that your prospects of beating Dr Lloyd are jolly good.' Her eyes followed the blond doctor's progress through the pool. 'Given a few weeks' practice, I think that you'd give him a good swim for his money; don't you agree, Babs?'

'Oh, absolutely,' replied Babs, returning Jane's rather forced smile.

She was conscious of a little shiver of disquiet washing over her. Somehow she had briefly upset her colleague, though how or why she had no idea. Could it have been because of the tough but, in the event, effective attack she had made on Colin? Or was Jane offended because a brand-new member of staff had succeeded in getting him interested in swimming when she and others, such as Guy Lloyd, on his own admission, had failed? Surely not; Jane was too much of a professional for that. She would welcome anything that improved her patient's chances.

The rest of the morning passed uneventfully, and Jane seemed pleasant enough, so that Babs began to wonder if she had imagined the flash of dislike in the physio's eyes earlier.

It was lunchtime when they finished working their way through the list of patients for treatment. To Babs's surprise, Jane said, as they were about to part, 'You and I seem to work well together as a team; perhaps Sister Crewe would let us do so on a regular basis. I'm sure it's much better for the patients to be helped by the same people all the time.'

Babs was delighted by the suggestion, for it certainly meant that Jane didn't hold any sort of grudge against her. 'I couldn't agree more. I'll ask Sister this afternoon if that's possible,' she said, beaming with pleasure, and on that happy note she and Jane parted.

Sister Crewe professed herself only too pleased to rota them as a team; it was the sort of rapport she wanted to establish in the department. It was because the unit was a new one, with fresh ideas about the treatment of post-trauma patients of all conditions and ages, that the physios and nursing staff worked so closely together. In many hospitals physios simply asked for help from the busy nursing staff when they couldn't manage alone; here at Princes Park they intended reversing that casual approach, and going all-out for teamwork, with everyone from consultants downwards co-operating.

As overall head of the department, it was up to Sister Crewe to see that this happened. In the space of three days Babs had learned to admire the unit sister, with her ability to persuade professionals from all the different disciplines to work together harmoniously. It was an achievement to get a whole lot of highly trained people to pool their resources without their feeling that they were losing their own identity of purpose.

To foster this co-operation, Sister Crewe had organised a weekly meeting of all those connected with the unit. This included consultants as well as the regular medics, physios, nurses and technicians working in

rehab. This week's meeting was arranged for seven
o'clock on the evening of Babs's fourth day at Princes.

Brilliant organiser that she was, Sister Crewe, or
Angela, as she liked to be called off duty, had turned
the working meetings into social get-togethers, knowing that virtually everyone was giving up their free time
to be there. By making it a casual, out-of-uniform
affair, she hoped for, and got, a high level of interest
and input.

A mingling and exchange of ideas was encouraged
before the meeting got properly under way, and a
buffet spread was laid on.

Having arrived in good time, Babs was finding the
experience of mixing with all layers of the hospital
hierarchy fascinating. Angela Crewe introduced her to
several people connected with the unit whom she had
not yet met, and then suggested that she should try the
buffet before the meeting started.

Babs was only too ready to eat, having skipped tea,
and was on the point of choosing something from the
laden table when she felt a man's hand on her shoulder.
She thought, with a little leap of pleasure, that it was
Guy Lloyd who had sought her out. She turned to
speak, a ready smile on her face, and discovered, with
a stab of disappointment, that it was not Guy, but the
grey-haired Roger Mansfield who was standing behind
her.

His appearance surprised her. The last time she'd
seen him, when he had given her a lift, he had been
wearing a beautifully tailored pale grey suit, and crisp
collar and tie. Now he was still well turned out, but in
a casual manner, in white designer jeans and an open-

necked shirt. He looked younger, in spite of his grey, receding hair; he was perhaps in his mid-thirties.

'It's Babs, isn't it?' he said. She was surprised; she had thought that he was too cold and stiff to use the diminutive of her name. 'How are you settling in?'

Babs swallowed. 'Oh, fine, Mr Mansfield, thank you. Everyone is so kind, helping me find my feet, as it were. And the set-up is terrific.'

She was even more surprised when he put a finger to his lips, and said, with a supercilious smile, 'No "Mr"s tonight; Angela insists on informality at these little functions.' His voice was heavy with sarcasm.

Oh,' said Babs, her dark brown eyes widening and glowing with fun. 'Somebody said that it was all Christian names, but somehow I didn't think that extended to grand folk like senior registrars.'

'My dear girl, Angela's word is a law that even superior beings like consultants comply with.' He added, sounding even more sarcastic, 'We're all boys and girls together tonight, for our sins. It's Tom, Dick and Mary all round.'

Babs wondered why he had come, since he seemed to disapprove so strongly. What a sarcastic devil he is, she thought. She wished that she could get away from him, but couldn't think how to do it without seeming rude.

Perhaps her feelings were showing in her face, for he said suddenly, 'Look, why don't you go and grab us a couple of chairs over there by the window, while I collect some grub. Just tell me if there's anything that you can't stomach among this lot.' He waved his hand over the table.

'I can eat anything,' said Babs, relieved at his change of attitude. 'Nothing upsets me. Just pile on the stuff; I'm starving.'

Roger wrinkled his nose. 'Oh, yes, I remember — sticky cream buns.'

'But I do take lots of exercise and clean my teeth after meals.'

'Yes, so you said. Well, so do I, but I keep off the obvious killers to teeth and arteries, and I too take plenty of exercise, when I've time. Now please go and grab those chairs before someone else does.'

Reluctantly Babs did as he suggested. She didn't want to spend the evening in his company, but she didn't seem to have much choice. She had just sat down and put her cardigan on the spare chair to claim it when Guy and Jane appeared almost beside her, coming through the doors leading from the sun-drenched terrace. At the sight of Guy her heart missed a beat.

He was holding Jane's hand, and they were both looking cool and slightly damp. It was obvious that they had been swimming. The back of Guy's hair, where it had got wetter constantly, was quite dark compared to the bleached blond of the rest of his white-gold cap. They both smiled at her. Guy's dazzling blue eyes were warm and very friendly, and he seemed pleased to see her.

'Hi, Babs, thank goodness we're not late for Angela's shindig,' he said. 'Or food,' he added. 'God, I'm starving. Can we get you anything while we're getting ours?'

Jane said sharply, 'Guy, I'm sure Babs doesn't need

our help; she obviously has someone looking after her.'
She indicated the cardigan on the spare chair. 'Why do
you think she's saving a chair?'

Babs, annoyed by Jane's sharp tone, and the proprie-
torial way she was clasping Guy's hand, said with
determined brightness, 'Jane's quite right, Guy, thank
you. I'm being very well looked after by Roger; he's
collecting food right now.'

'Do you mean Roger Mansfield?' asked Jane and
Guy in unison, in surprised voices.

'The one and only,' said Roger in an acid voice from
behind them. He handed Babs a laden plate, with a
glass of wine balanced on it, and sat down with his own
plate and wine.

Jane tugged at Guy's hand. 'Come on,' she said, in a
pleased fashion, giving Babs a wide smile. 'Let's leave
these two to it, and get something to eat before the
food's all gone.'

'Yes, of course, love.' He smiled at Babs and Roger.
'See you two later.'

Babs felt a wave of resentment sweep over her. Jane
had deliberately made a point of stressing the fact that
she and Roger were together, and Guy had endorsed it
with his parting words. Well, she told herself, it's your
own fault; you made a thing of being with someone
that you've only got yourself to blame.

'As couples go, they make a nice-looking pair,' said
Roger in a cool, appraising sort of voice as Guy and
Jane walked away.

'Yes, they do,' returned Babs shortly, and then,
realising how brusque she sounded, and afraid of

arousing Roger's suspicions, added in a brighter tone, 'The proverbial perfect match.'

She expected him to make a sarcastic remark disagreeing with her, but to her surprise he didn't.

'That's true,' he said, taking a sip of wine. 'Guy's good at his job — he'll go far, I dare say — and from what I've heard Jane's a good physio.' He shrugged. 'If medical men must get married, at least it makes sense to stick to somebody who understands that the job must come first.'

For some reason, much of the shine had gone out of the evening. She had been looking forward to this first get-together of all those involved in the rehab unit and felt happy that she was part of a team connected with this unique experiment in patient rehabilitation. So what had happened to dull her pleasure? Could it be Jane's sharpness when they had greeted each other, or the way she had made it plain that Guy was her property, a suggestion underlined by Roger commenting on their attractiveness as a pair?

Babs didn't know the answer to any of these questions. She only knew that suddenly she felt depressed, or perhaps not so much depressed as lonely, lost here among a host of strangers, however kind and helpful. She was homesick for her parents and family, and the wilds of the border country far to the north.

She heaved a great sigh and reminded herself that she had deliberately come down here to the south to work at this new and inspirational rehabilitation centre. Once she had done a stint here she would be able to return north and head her own department, and make it as famous as Princes Park. The thought cheered her and she looked up to smile at Roger, only to find that he was staring intently at her with his cold grey eyes. If only they had been Guy's warm blue ones, she thought, she wouldn't feel lonely.

Had Roger spoken and she not heard him? It was possible; she had been so deep in thought. She started to mumble an apology, but he interrupted.

'Are you all right?' he asked brusquely. 'You looked miles away and you almost stopped eating, which was quite worrying, considering your appetite.'

Babs felt that she owed him an explanation. 'I was thinking about home,' she said. 'Isn't it silly? I've lived away from home for years — at school, then training in London — but every so often I get homesick.'

'Where's home?'

'Cumbria.'

'Ah, I'm from rather further on than that.'

'Where?'

'Just north of Inverness.'

'You're a Scot.'

'For my sins.'

'My mother's a Scot, but from the west coast — Ayr.'

They had found a topic of interest that would have kept them occupied for some time, if at that moment Angela hadn't called the meeting to order.

Much of the discussion was about patients' progress before Babs had joined the staff, and she listened with interest, but some detachment. It gave her a chance to study her colleagues as they listened or contributed to the discussion. As the registrar in sole charge of the unit, Guy was brought into the debate a good deal, answering questions, put mostly by the consultants about their patients, and concerning their day-to-day treatment, for which he was responsible. His answers were always lucid, and to the point. He certainly knew his stuff.

'You seem to have made a breakthrough, Guy, with Colin Newbry,' said John Carter, who had several times operated on the young paraplegic after he'd had his accident that had left him paralysed from the waist downwards. 'A great improvement after his sessions in the pool. Congratulations on persuading him to give it a try at last.'

'That wasn't my doing,' said Guy, looking across to where Babs was sitting. 'It was all down to our new staff nurse, Barbara Becker-Brown.'

The consultant and almost everyone else in the room looked at Babs. 'Ah,' said John Carter. 'So you're the Bossy Boots Colin spoke of.' He beamed at her. 'You gave him quite a rollicking, I hear. Well done.'

'Jane and I were working together. . .' said Babs, rather overwhelmed at being singled out. 'It was a combined effort.' She felt herself blushing, but it was less because of the consultant's praise than because Guy was looking so pleased. It was ludicrous, she told herself, to read so much into an exchange of glances in a roomful of people, but the idea persisted that Guy was pleased with her, and for her.

Roger, when she caught his eye, was looking at her thoughtfully. 'You must tell me some time,' he said, 'what magic you worked to get that particular young man into the pool. He's been dead against it for weeks.'

'Oh, are you interested in Colin?'

'Not specifically any more, but he was in our unit for

a while when he had a viral infection that affected his heart. He's stabilised on medication now, but he went through a bad patch following the trauma of his accident and near cardiac failure. Swimming in the right environment should help all round.'

The meeting broke up soon after this and everyone started to drift out into the summer night, in pairs or small groups. Babs wondered how she could politely extricate herself from what might be an embarrassing situation with Roger Mansfield. It hadn't been too bad talking to him at the meeting, but she didn't think that he would want to continue the exercise, and she certainly didn't. She found him too caustic, and downright sarcastic. He was an uncomfortable companion. It was just as Roger was caught up in conversation with one of the consultants that Guy, followed by Jane, appeared at her side.

'We're going over to the clubhouse for a drink, and a game of darts,' said Guy cheerfully. 'Thought you might like to come.'

'As a foursome,' added Jane quickly. 'With Roger.'

'Oh.' Babs looked at Roger, who was standing a few feet away, talking to his colleague. 'I don't know about Roger. He probably has other plans, but I'd love to come.'

Jane said firmly, 'I bet any plans that he has include you, Babs. Don't be coy.'

Babs didn't know what to make of this remark. It almost seemed as if Jane was determined to read something significant into the fact that the registrar had sat with her during the meeting. She didn't have time to wonder further, or think of how to reply to Jane's remark, as Roger finished his conversation, and moved over to join the three of them.

'We were just suggesting to Babs that you two might like to join us in the clubhouse,' said Guy.

'Good idea. Shall we do that?' He looked at Babs enquiringly, and as if he was really interested in knowing what she wanted to do.

Babs was in a quandary. She didn't want to spend any more of the evening in his company and had expected him to feel the same and refuse Guy's invitation, but he had dumped the decision back on her. Perhaps she should invent a prior engagement or use the hoary old excuse that her hair needed a shampoo, but the exciting thought of spending a few hours in Guy's company, even with the possessive Jane, proved too enticing.

She threw caution to the wind, and said gaily, 'It's fine by me; I like a good game of darts.'

The room by then was almost empty, and the four of them left, with Guy and Roger leading the way through the rhododendron walk, shady now in the late but still hot evening sunshine. Jane and Babs followed behind. Guy, thought Babs, looked like a wounded hero returned from the wars, limping along with his support-bandaged ankle and stick. He was casually dressed in fawn denims and a white T-shirt, which clung to his bronzed torso like a second skin.

But it wasn't just Guy's splended physique, Babs acknowledged as the four of them approached the clubhouse, that she found so attractive, it was the enigmatic quality that he conveyed. There was an air about him, cool and authoritative, beneath the friendly, open personality. It made him in a way more of an enigma, because it was unexpected. At the meeting this evening he had spoken with firmness and knowledge, and it was clear that his views concerning the patients on the rehab unit were much respected by everyone. He was a man, and a doctor, to be reckoned with, she decided, not least because he carried his air of command lightly and pleasantly. He was of a greater substance than a casual acquaintanceship might suggest. Beneath the masculine good looks lay a strong character, a man who knew what he wanted, a natural leader, a man to be obeyed.

CHAPTER THREE

THE following morning Babs got up early to have a swim, though she was not on duty till two o'clock. She felt happy and accepted into Princes' social life, after last night's meeting and the subsequent hour spent with Jane, Guy and Roger in the clubhouse.

They'd had a friendly game of darts, with Guy making much of the fact that his injured ankle stopped him playing with his usual skill. Any antagonism that Jane might have felt towards Babs earlier in the evening had quite vanished by the time they all parted for the night, Jane and a limping Guy going off in one direction to pick up Jane's car, and Roger escorting Babs to the staff quarters.

Although it had been by then nearly eleven o'clock, there was still a faint glow of daylight in the western sky.

'If we were at home in Scotland,' Roger had said, 'it would still be light enough to read on a June night like this.'

'But Scotland isn't my home,' said Babs, 'although I go there quite a bit to stay with my grandparents. My home is in Cumbria, remember?'

'Don't split hairs, lassie. You ken fine what I mean.'

His levity surprised her; he seemed too cold a man to make even a mild joke.

33

'You hide your accent very well most of the time,' she said.

He pulled a face. 'English schools,' he said laconically.

'Well, you're nay so bad for all that,' replied Babs, in an excruciating Scottish accent.

He actually laughed, enabling them to part without embarrassment, wishing each other a friendly good-night when they reached the nurses' home.

Lying in bed later, Babs found herself comparing Roger with Guy. Roger was a handsome but cold man, caustic with his tongue, and old in manner if not in years. He was respected by his colleagues, but was not close to any of them. He lacked warmth.

Guy was the very opposite. He had tremendous charisma, strengthened by the fact that glimpsed beneath the handsome exterior was a strong, rather arrogant character who knew exactly what he wanted and would get it. This quality added to his attractions, and most of the females with whom he came into contact would have given much to be in the privileged position which seemed to be held by Jane. What was she to him? wondered Babs. And what was he to her? There was no doubt that a strong rapport existed between them, but how deep was it, and was it evenly reciprocated? Even being with them all evening, it was difficult to judge. Jane had made no secret about her feelings for Guy, but if he had any special feelings for Jane he had kept them to himself.

Babs recalled those moments during the evening when she had felt Guy's eyes upon her, but had resisted meeting his gaze even though she had wanted to return

it. Once or twice he had brushed against her, and she
had been very conscious of his closeness, but had
deliberately held herself aloof. She hoped that he
wasn't aware of the effect he was having on her.
Instinct warned her not to give Jane any cause to
suspect her of being remotely interested in Guy, or it
would spoil the successful working partnership that
they were establishing between them.

Anyway, on her own account, she must suppress this
ridiculous feeling that she had of being drawn towards
Guy. No way was she going to tolerate distractions that
stood in the way of her career. Her career was the
important factor. Time for romance and commitment
later. The handsome Guy Lloyds of this world she was
determined to ignore.

On this resolution, she had willed herself to sleep.

The plastic-domed staff pool was empty when she
arrived for her swim at seven, and there was a wonderful feeling of space about it. The morning was already
hot, and it was heaven to slip into the cool, silky
softness of the water.

She raced up and down the length of the pool, doing
breast-stroke, crawl, and, on the third length, backstroke. She was a few metres into the third length when
she realised that she was not alone. Another swimmer
had entered the pool and was catching her up. She
increased the speed of her strokes, knowing that she
had plenty of speed and power left in her. The other
swimmer must have done likewise, because she could
actually see a blur of movement as she swam. She
struggled to find more power, but knew that she had

now reached her maximum, discovering this just as the
other contestant drew abreast of her. Through the
sparkling drops of water she recognised Guy Lloyd,
and her heart lurched with pleasure. Her smooth
rhythm faltered, and with a few more powerful strokes
he overtook her, shooting past in a ripple and froth of
water.

Babs recovered herself, and almost caught up with
him, touching the end of the pool a metre or so behind
him. He waited for her to get her breath and wipe the
water from her face, and run her hand through her
short, crisp tawny-coloured hair.

'Thanks,' he said. 'That's the best race I've had in
ages. You were brilliant. One of the few things we're
short of here at Princes is good swimmers.'

Babs was thrilled by the compliment and Guy's
nearness. She felt herself blushing, and strove to be
sensible.

'Well, I had a head start.'

'Not as much as you'd be given in an official mixed
race. You weren't far along when I entered the pool.'
Guy looked at her admiringly, his blue eyes sweeping
over her with interest. 'You've got a great backstroke,'
he insisted.

Quite unaware of how attractive she looked with her
water-spangled hair smoothed back from her small,
square-chinned face and her laughing brown eyes, Babs
said, 'I bet backstroke is your weakest stroke; it
happens to be almost my best, so it's not surprising
that I did quite well against you.' She was determined
not to be seeming to seek any favours because of her

sex, nor to be over-feminist, but just wanted him to see that she was being fair.

'What is your best stroke, Babs?' His voice was deep, like velvet; his blue eyes were fixed on her, his strong, proud face serious.

'Butterfly.'

'Right, now that really is my worst, so, to make it all fair and square, taking into account male and female muscle and so on, supposing you have a six-metre start over two lengths? How does that grab you?'

Obviously he understood her unspoken thoughts about not being patronised. 'A six-metre start sounds fine,' she said. Then remembered about his ankle. He was wearing a tubigrip sock. 'Will you be able to get a good push-off?' she asked.

'I'll be fine.' He walked round the side of the pool, limping very slightly, but otherwise his usual fit, athletic self. His bronzed leg and back muscles glistened with water as he moved. Babs watched him, fascinated. 'Shall we say that the six-metre mark is here?' he said, stopping by one of the loops in the side-rope. She nodded. 'Right, I'll follow on when you reach here. As we haven't got an observer around you'll just have to trust me, Babs.' He smiled, and her heart seemed to flip over.

She watched him, mesmerised by the power and beauty of his body, as he walked back round the pool. His eyes were on her as he approached. They met hers as he came to a halt beside her. Apart from the faint slapping of the water on the pool sides, it was very quiet under the translucent dome. Muted sunlight glittered on the water, and the reflected light played on their wet bodies.

He broke the silence at last, saying in a soft, low drawl, 'Babs, you look stunning, quite stunning.' He put out a hand and touched her arm, and ran his index finger up and down her pale gold skin. She quivered beneath his touch. This can't be happening to me, she thought. What was he saying? He smiled, and said in his natural low-pitched voice, 'You look so right in a swimsuit — perfect.'

'Oh,' murmured Babs, half laughing with disbelief and a breathless excitement.

Guy's eyes continued to bore into hers. His hands gripped the soft upper parts of her arms. 'You're lovely,' he breathed, 'quite lovely.'

She shook like a leaf at his touch. It was ridiculous. He couldn't mean it; he was just flirting with her. She knew that her white costume stretched over her small, high breasts, enhanced her tanned, slim body, but was amazed that he should use the word 'lovely'. She might be attractive, but stunning, lovely? Surely that was over the top.

It was hard to believe that this was happening, that the tall, silver-blond, handsome Guy Lloyd was saying such things to her.

There was a sound from the other end of the pool, and a voice — Roger Mansfield's voice — was wishing them a steely, 'Good morning.'

Babs froze, though why she had no idea. Did it matter if Roger had heard or seen anything that had passed between herself and Guy? Of course it didn't; not that he could have heard much from the other end of the pool. And yet she felt almost guilty for having responded to Guy so obviously, for letting him affect her so strongly. Not that it was anyone's business but hers and Guy's, she told herself, except possibly, she admitted reluctantly, Jane's.

Guy recovered himself without seeming effort. He gave Babs's arms a reassuring squeeze, before casually removing his hands. 'We were just setting up a race,' he called down the length of the pool. 'Will you umpire, Roger?'

'Sure,' said Roger in a bored voice. 'What do you want me to do?'

'Babs is to have a six-metre start in a butterfly race. The six-metre mark is here.' He indicated the point which they had agreed upon. 'Will you start us both off at the appropriate time?'

'Will do.' Roger made his way down the poolside towards them. He looked very thin and pale compared to Guy, but he didn't look unfit.

With a determined effort Babs put behind her the little scene with Guy, and concentrated on the race. It had suddenly assumed a great importance, become a test of some sort, in which she had to prove herself. It had more to do with her growing attraction towards Guy than a simple fun swim. Crossly she damped down her silly thoughts. It was just a friendly race.

Even with a fair start, she knew that she was going to have to fight hard to keep a lead over Guy, who she fancied was up to county standards. Well, she had swum for her school and her county in junior events in the past, and had kept up her practice as far as possible in later years. She would certainly match Guy, for effort at least.

Roger arrived at their end of the pool. 'Ready when you are,' he said in his strange, impersonal fashion.

Babs poised herself for her launch into the pool.

'On the count of three,' said Roger. 'One, two, three.'

She took a great leap into the water, giving herself as much of a start as possible, and then began the rhythmic arm and leg movements to propel herself along as fast as possible. She was concentrating so hard that she wasn't sure how far Guy was behind her, until she had completed one length; then, as she made a smooth, fast turn, she saw that he was still several metres in the rear. She was holding her own. The knowledge made her put in that little extra effort, so that she seemed to half swim, half fly through the water. They touched the poolside together.

They were both breathing hard, but it wasn't just on account of the race; it was something to do with being near each other in the clear aquamarine water.

'My God,' Guy said softly. 'You literally flew along; I only just caught up with you.'

They blinked water out of their eyes as they looked at each other. Guy's eyes were full of deep admiration and something deeper.

He put out a hand and touched her shoulder. 'Babs,' he murmured.

Roger's voice broke in from above their heads, shattering the moment. Guy let his hand drop to his side.

'Well done, Babs,' said Roger. 'Congratulations.

Guy had to work like a Trojan to catch up. Now, if you've finished, I'll do a few lengths before duty calls.' He dived neatly into the pool and, with a few smooth strokes, powered himself through the water with an easy crawl.

Guy climbed out of the pool and he leaned down to pull her from the water, dragging her wet body against his. Babs felt as if she were melting into him; their bare thighs were touching. He was hard with desire, and she soft, moist, yielding, as his hands, firm on the small of her back, kept her pressed against him. Her erect nipples were squashed bruisingly hard against his muscular chest. He looked down at her, his blue eyes smouldering. She was longing for him to kiss her. She lifted her face.

He made a smothered exclamation, and put her from him in one smooth movement.

'No,' he said in a low, harsh voice. 'I must be mad.' He stepped away from her. He stood there staring at her for a few moments. Then in a flat, unemotional voice he said, 'That shouldn't have happened. I'm sure that neither of us wants this. Let's get changed.' He turned and walked towards the cubicles.

Babs stood there immobile by the edge of the pool. She felt as if she had been kicked by something hard; there was a pain and a soreness in her stomach. She felt sick. Muddled, unpleasant, humiliating thoughts raced through her head as she watched Guy walk away from her. How could she have let herself get into this mess, allowed him to reject her, humiliate her? She knew that she should have been on guard against him; she'd warned herself. How could she have been so stupid as to forget all that the moment he had touched her?

Through the thunder of her tumultuous thoughts, she heard Roger swimming back up the pool. He mustn't see her like this; he mustn't guess at anything that had happened. Blindly blinking back tears, she turned and made for the showers.

She paddled through the foot-hygiene pool, kicking at the water, trying to kick away her unhappy thoughts, trying to pretend that nothing of importance had happened. She and Guy had simply been attracted by chemistry to each other, and he, quite rightly, had drawn back before it was too late.

In spite of the sultry heat that threw a dusty haze over the parkland, she went for a long jog round the periphery of the extensive grounds after picking unhappily at her breakfast.

All the while she was running she went over and over in her mind the events in the swimming-pool. She knew that for her own sake, and Guy's, and Jane's, she must squash her feelings for Guy. The fact that no other man had affected her the way he had meant nothing. It was just chemistry. After all, she hardly knew him; she couldn't possibly be in love with him, or he with her. Things didn't happen like that in real life.

By the time she was getting ready to go on duty she had talked some sort of sense into herself. It was as well that things had turned out the way they had, she decided, before she had got too deeply involved. She wasn't going to let anything or anyone divert her from her career plans. This morning's episode had been a little hiccup, nothing more. She wouldn't, she just wouldn't let herself be miserable over what had happened, and she certainly wouldn't give Guy any reason to believe that he had hurt her. Next time she saw him she would greet him quite calmly, as if nothing had happened.

In fact it was some days before she saw Guy again, except to catch fleeting glimpses of him in passing. He was terribly busy on other wards, and her duty periods and his visits to the unit seldom coincided.

To her relief, she and Jane went on working together as before. It was clear from Jane's conversation that she knew nothing about any rift between Guy and Babs, which wasn't surprising, though she did know that they had had a race in the pool one morning, with Roger present. The fact that Roger had been there seemed to reassure Jane. She was determined to see Babs and Roger as a pair, which Babs found annoying, but at the same time convenient. If Jane thought that, then presumably Guy did too, which would make it easier to conceal her true feelings.

It was four days later when Babs and Guy met. Babs was entering the refectory as Guy was leaving. She felt the blood rush to her face, and a wave of giddiness for a moment threatened to overwhelm her as they almost collided in the doorway. But she recovered quickly, managed a tight smile, and muttered a good morning.

In reply, he pulled a face — an unshaven face, she realised, as he stood back to let her come through the door, which probably meant that he had been on duty since the early hours. Briefly he gave her a long, searching, enigmatic look that could mean anything, but his voice, when he spoke, was quite cheerful and normal.

'Bleeped again,' he said, 'or we might have shared breakfast. Pity, but I've got to dash; something of a crisis brewing, with which only Superman Guy Lloyd can deal.' He assumed an American accent. 'I can tell you, kid, it's hard work being a superhero.' His tired smile grew broader; his bright blue eyes twinkled with amusement. It was as if nothing had happened between them.

Babs was for a moment struck dumb. She had dreaded this meeting and had expected that he would, like her, be embarrassed. Instead, he was being mature and sophisticated, and ignoring what had happened. Mentally she shook herself. She was glad that he was treating this meeting lightly. They had to work together, and forget the emotional near-incident in the pool. Personal concerns couldn't be allowed to get in the way of their duty to their patients.

She willed herself to say in the same teasing fashion as his, 'Then I mustn't delay you. On your way, Superman.'

For a moment she fancied that Guy's eyes flared with a gleam of admiration, or perhaps it was relief at her reaction.

He shrugged his broad shoulders, and said with wry humour, 'Well, mustn't stand here all day exchanging small talk when my country needs me. Farewell, see you anon.' He sketched a small bow, raised a hand in salute, and moved swiftly away.

'*Au revoir*, Superman,' murmured Babs as she watched his receding figure. She smiled to herself; she couldn't believe what had happened. Guy had turned the meeting that she had dreaded, and had expected to be an embarrassment, into a light-hearted encounter. She was well aware that nothing had basically changed between them; she had made a fool of herself, and he had rejected her — nothing could alter that — but somehow he had taken charge of matters, and made them bearable. Now she would be able to meet him on equal terms. It was quite an achievement. She swallowed her pride, and acknowledged that he really was quite an extraordinary man.

It was a blessing that the rehabilitation unit was reasonably quiet, with the quota of resident patients dropping as several were discharged home, and visiting patients from wards and home remaining static. This meant that their ongoing programmes of treatment were already processed, and the physios, nurses and other auxiliary staff could carry on with their work without constant assessment from Guy.

The situation began to change by the end of the week, with several admissions from various wards in the hospital, which was beginning to fill up with summer visitors needing urgent treatment. Sister Crewe forecast that the unit would soon be full up.

She was right. By the following Wednesday, all twenty ward beds were occupied by patients in varying stages of rehabilitation. Most were due to go home in a short while and were learning how to deal, in a domestic situation, with their disability. This meant that Babs was kept busy much of the time in the 'home unit'. This was a specially constructed annexe to the main building, consisting of a sitting-room-cum-dining-room, a kitchen, bathroom and lavatory. Patients considered fit enough spent whole days in the unit, cooking and cleaning for themselves, and even taking showers and baths under supervision of a staff nurse, and/or a physiotherapist or occupational therapist.

On this particular afternoon Babs was working on her own. Jane had gone off to perform some particularly complicated physiotherapy on an orthopaedic patient in the ward, leaving Babs to cope with a stroke lady and a double below-knee amputee in a wheelchair in the Home Unit. It was all quite normal, except that today both Ken Brown, the amputee, and Iris Lomax, the elderly stroke lady, wanted to use the kitchen at the same time, one to make a cup of coffee, the other to make a cake.

Perhaps it was the hot weather making both patients irritable, thought Babs, looking longingly across the stretch of sun-scorched grass at the hydrotherapy pool, and wishing that she were on duty there.

'Mrs Lomax,' she pleaded, 'please let Ken make his coffee before you start on your cake; it'll only take a few minutes, whereas your cake will take some time to prepare.'

'I was here first,' replied Mrs Lomax, her slurred words very determined. 'I put on the list that I wanted to use the kitchen this afternoon. If Ken can't read, that's his look-out. He only had to ask, but no, he just barged in and insisted that he put the kettle on for his coffee.'

She was right in a way, thought Babs. The list was there for all to see, and Iris had booked the kitchen

from three to four. Ken ought to have seen and
respected that, or asked her permission to make his
coffee, not insisted upon it. There certainly wasn't
room in the small kitchen for a large wheelchair and a
tottery old lady. She would have to do something.

'Look,' she said, feeling rather desperate in the face
of the implacable fronts that both patients were showing. 'I could do with a cup of coffee or tea; supposing I
make some for the three of us? Then you can take
yours out on the patio, Ken, and read your *Rev Up*
magazine, while we get on with our cake making.'

Ken was quite agreeable to this solution, and so,
after a few minutes of bridling with indignation, was
Iris Lomax.

Babs heaved a sigh of relief as both patients made
their way back to the sitting-room, leaving her to make
the drinks.

'Do you think you could make that four cups?' said
Guy's voice from the doorway. 'I'm simply gasping for
a cuppa.'

Babs felt the familiar wave of pleasure at seeing him
sweep over her, but suppressed it immediately. 'You're
welcome, Doctor,' she said in a deliberately low-key
voice.

Guy looked at her thoughtfully. 'Are you pleased to
see me, Babs?' he asked, and added, 'Strictly as a
friend and colleague.'

She met his gaze without flinching, though with an
effort. In spite of all her good resolutions, she still felt
uneasy in his presence, and yet the last thing she
wanted was for him to go away. He was here, throwing
her off balance, making her feel strange, detached

from her surroundings. It was ludicrous. She must get
a hold on herself.

'Of course I'm pleased to see you,' she said, wishing
that she didn't sound so defensive. She waved a hand
round the empty kitchen. 'Everyone on the unit has
missed you; we are all pleased to see you again.'

'I'm glad to hear it,' he said laconically. 'A case
perhaps of absence making the heart grow fonder?'

They were on dangerous ground; the conversation
was becoming full of innuendoes.

'Well, old proverbs are often the truest,' she said
with a stilted laugh. 'And Sister Crewe certainly misses
you; she said so this morning.'

'Well, I'm glad about that,' Guy said drily. He
pointed a finger towards the kettle, which was bubbling
merrily. 'Water's boiling, I think, Staff. Don't you
think that you should make the tea?'

Babs, trying to conceal shaking hands, made several
mugs of tea and coffee.

'By the way,' she said, forcing herself to sound calm,
'I see that you and Jane are entering for the mixed
doubles in the club tennis match. Roger has asked me
to partner him.'

'And. . .?'

'I'm thinking it over. You and Jane will take some
beating, from what I've heard.'

'I can tell you that Roger is no mean player.'

'So I believe.'

'You'll make a good pair.'

'Do you think so?'

'Oh, yes, you'll complement each other splendidly.
Opposites sometimes do that, don't they?' His

expression was unreadable, but Babs felt that he was implying something, though what it was she had no idea.

'Yes, they do,' said Babs. 'I think I'll take him up on the offer.'

'You could do worse.'

Yes, thought Babs, and I could do a whole lot better with you, Guy, if only I knew what you really thought. If only I knew how you feel about Jane. If only I weren't absolutely bent on carving out a career for myself in nursing. But I am, and it's just as well that Jane's around to keep an eye on you, because I don't want to be committed to anyone, not even you.

CHAPTER FOUR

BABS found the next few weeks both exciting and trying in almost equal measure. She was seeing Guy and Roger daily, either at work or at tennis practice, and occasionally in the swimming-pool. She tried very hard to view Guy simply as a friend and colleague, but the very thought of seeing him each morning sent her to work on wings. She told herself that it didn't matter, so long as he, or Jane, was not aware of the effect he had on her, and also that it did not affect her work.

On this score she was on firm ground. She and Jane continued to work together with patients, and there did seem to be evidence after a while that their combined regular efforts were paying dividends.

Sister Crewe was delighted. 'This is the sort of thing that makes Princes unique with rehabilitation,' she said one day, when Ken Brown, the amputee who had always been rather truculent and aggressive, had actually praised the efforts of Babs and Jane. He was about to be discharged home for a few weeks, but would be returning later to have new limbs fitted.

'They've been really patient with me, Sister,' he'd said, 'making me do my exercises when I should, looking after my stumps and making sure that they don't get sore, and finding out about that bloke who designs model bikes. I mean, I didn't expect them to do things like that, when it's just to stop me getting bored out of my skull. I spoke to him the other day on the phone. He's coming to see me soon.'

'I'm so pleased, Ken. That's what we're here for — to help make life more interesting, fuller.'

'Well, they've certainly done that, and from my point of view one of the best things has been that I always have the same people looking after me. It makes a hell of a difference, you know. They get to understand about all the little things that are important, like where you like your papers put, and which cushion you like to sit on. Small things, but very important. Mind you, it was a bonus for me, being looked after by the two prettiest birds on the block.' He winked at Sister Crewe. 'Though looking at you, Sister, I've got to admit that you're all a pretty stunning lot on this unit; even Doc Lloyd's quite something, as blokes go.'

'It's high time you were off home, my man,' said Sister, pretending to be severe. 'You're a corrupting influence on my staff.'

Guy was busy on the unit these days, with lots of examinations to do and assessments to make on admissions and discharges. Jane made no secret of the fact that having him around when she was working was a bonus. His presence added a glow to her already pretty face and a zest to her work.

On Babs it had a mixed effect after the first thrill of seeing him each morning subsided. She was conscious of his presence and the feeling of being drawn to him almost against her will. She honestly wanted to make nursing her career, and had no intention of fouling it up by committing herself to a serious relationship, but the effect he had on her was disturbing. Fight it, she told herself over and over again; surely you're capable of just being friends with the man?

For the most part she was able to convince herself that it was sufficient to be one of the tennis foursome that she and Roger and Jane and Guy seemed to have become. It was safe that way, and she could enjoy Guy's company without fear of becoming too involved. The set-up, she almost convinced herself, was ideal. In time this overwhelming desire that she had to fling herself into Guy's arms and feel him thrusting against her, as he had at the poolside, would fade. It's all hormonal, she told herself through gritted teeth.

It was just as well that Jane was around, so clearly in love with Guy. Every word or gesture that she spoke or made in connection with him implied deep and genuine affection. What was not so clear was how Guy felt about Jane. That was still a mystery. Superficially he was cheerfully affectionate, holding her hand when they walked together, flinging a casual arm round her shoulder in a way that made Babs sick with envy, and teasing her with the kind of intimacy that built up naturally in a close relationship. But how close, how vital? It was impossible to know.

There were wonderful moments when Babs thought that Guy was as conscious of her as she was of him. . . a glance that made her breathless, an accidental touch that made her tremble with a sensuous delight, eager for more. But the moments passed, and, looking at his tanned, handsome face that she longed to touch, she could see nothing there that betrayed any such feelings, and she always reached the same frustrating conclusion: that she had been imagining his reaction to her.

The poolside episode had obviously been a one-off which he regretted. It had been important to her, but not to him, and he found it easy to put it behind him, for the sake of his career, and perhaps some vague future plans involving Jane.

He was very ambitious, and the last thing he would want was a commitment.

Well, so was she. She was enjoying her work immensely, and wanted to get on with it. She could do without this emotional turmoil. Thank God for Roger, with his acid tongue and jaundiced view of life. Tennis had pushed them into a partnership of sorts, and she was grateful for it.

She had occasional twinges of guilt concerning Roger. So many people said that they had never known him take time out of his studies until he started squiring her around. He was a workaholic, so what had she done to prise him away from his usual lifestyle? From her point of view, nothing. Roger had started seeking her out, and she, confused by her growing, but forbidden attraction for Guy, had accepted him in the few short weeks that she had been at Princes.

It might not last, but at present it suited her fine. She quelled her feelings of guilt that she was not giving much in return, and enjoyed his companionship.

Life in the unit got busier over those long, steamy summer days, with patients keeping the cubicle beds full. It seemed that there was a rush of people being discharged from the wards, being almost fit to go home, just needing help in Rehab with how to cope.

Babs went on duty one boilingly hot sunny morning, ten days after Elizabeth Pilbeam, whom she and Jane had been tending as a team, had been admitted from the cardio-thoracic unit, to learn that Jane was off sick.

Liz was a tricky case. Babs was particularly concerned that nothing should interfere with Liz's routine that she and Jane had established. The young woman was only eighteen, and had been badly burned in a fire. Smoke had affected her lungs, which was why she had been on Roger's unit, but they were now virtually back to normal; it was her scarred body and mind that was causing concern. She was waiting for skin grafts, and requiring intensive nursing, physiotherapy and psychiatric care. So far only Babs and Jane had made any headway and had succeeded in establishing a rapport with her, and gaining her confidence to some extent. It was vitally important that this rapport should not be broken.

Determined to prevent this, Babs spoke to Sister Crewe immediately after the report had been given.

'I would rather work on my own, with just help to move Liz when necessary,' she said, 'than subject her to a new physio. She's so conscious of her scarring, and has only just got to trust Jane and me not to hurt her too much. She's only having simple exercises, and effleurage massage to her limbs where possible. Jane has taught me this, and I'm quite capable of doing it on my own.'

'Well. . .' Sister sat back in her chair and considered. 'She is a rather special patient, which was why Mr

Mansfield wanted her moved to us rather early on. By rights she shouldn't have come to rehab for some time yet. But then that's what we're all about, isn't it? Looking after the whole person, bending the rules if it's necessary. I think you've got a point. You carry on till you need help, and I'll give you a hand personally.'

'Thanks, Sister, we'll both appreciate that.'

She went to say good morning to Liz and explain what was going to happen with her routine. Liz was sitting in the chair beside her bed, waiting for breakfast. She was propped up with carefully placed air cushions to keep the pressure off the still tender scarred areas on her left side, leg and arm. A large tear rolled down the side of her face as Babs entered the cubicle.

'I know,' she said, and more tears streamed down her cheeks. 'You've come to tell me who's going to take Jane's place this morning. I know she's off sick; the night staff told me.'

Babs slipped an arm round Liz's good shoulder. 'Well, that's all you know, funny face,' she said gently. 'I'm going to see to you on my own, as long as you're good and helpful, and Sister will give me a hand when I need it. Now how's that for service? Just wipe away those tears, and blow your nose, Liz, and I'll go and get your breakfast, and then we can get started.'

The relief on the girl's face was touching. She literally beamed at Babs; it was the best response from her yet.

As Babs came out of the cubicle she almost bumped into Guy, who was coming towards her, head down, examining a sheet of paper that he held in his hand. The sight of his white-blond hair made her heart flip and her cheeks flame with sudden pleasure. He looked up at that moment and saw Babs, and noted her flushed cheeks and the intense expression in her eyes, and his own eyes lit up and his face broke into a smile, his teeth gleaming against his bronzed tan.

Even as it was happening, she had the feeling that it had happened before. It was the swimming-pool incident all over again. The rattle of breakfast trays and the sound of voices faded. It was as if the two of them were alone in a shadowy landscape, just Guy and her.

They stood transfixed, drowning in each other's eyes, space between them lost. She didn't want to let this moment go. This was something that she had never experienced with anyone but Guy before, this wonderful, out-of-this-world coming together of their two innermost selves. This silent exchange of messages that had no need to be put into words.

Guy moved a step closer. He put out a hand and touched her arm, and her arm quivered, and her insides seemed to dissolve. 'Are you all right?' he asked, his voice coming from a great distance.

With a jerk she pulled herself together, let out her breath, which she seemed to have been holding for a long time, and whispered, 'Yes, I'm fine, thank you, fine.' She gave him a false, brilliant smile and asked innocently, 'How can I help you, Doctor? Do you want to see someone in particular?'

Guy said softly, gently teasing, 'I've seen someone in particular; now I want to see a patient, please — Mrs Rowe.'

'She's in cubicle five. I'm not sure if she's finished breakfast yet. I'll check.'

'Thank you.' There was now nothing in his voice to indicate what had just happened. He was simply the registrar in charge of the case, coming to assess a patient's progress.

Babs came out from the cubicle, carrying a tray. 'Mrs Rowe's finished her breakfast,' she said, her own voice cool, professional. 'I'll send a nurse to assist.'

For a moment she thought that Guy was going to insist that she be present, but he accepted what she had said, though his eyes meeting hers above the dishevelled breakfast tray seemed to say something different.

'Thank you, Staff.'

She tried to get a hold on herself and put Guy out of her mind. She wouldn't let herself dwell on the fact that this time he had responded, she hadn't imagined it, and he had teased her when she was trying to be cool and professional, as if he had wanted her to know that he had understood what had passed between them.

She took Liz's breakfast in to her and stayed, persuading her to eat, until she heard Guy leave the ward. He would be starting his rounds in the hospital now, checking on patients who were on the list to come to the rehabilitation unit in the near future. She was safe for a while.

Liz was hard work on her own. Babs missed Jane as she helped her special patient to shower, using an antiseptic skin-cleaning agent to make sure that none of the fragile burn areas became infected, but Liz's response made it worth while. At last, with Sister Crewe's help, she settled Liz on the massage couch in the treatment-room, and began the soothing strokes that massaged the circulation upwards towards the heart. She used an oil, especially made up in Pharmacy, which included a mild pain-killer to reduce the constant pain of the burnt tissues. It also contained a substance that the surgeons and pharmacologists thought might promote healing and generally improve the elasticity of the burnt areas, but it was in the experimental stage as yet.

Late morning Babs was due at the hydrotherapy pool to supervise Colin Newbry's swimming session. What a step forward it would be if she could persuade Liz to be wheeled there to see what was going on. So far she had refused to move further than the day-room, and then only when there was no one but staff around. Would I be pushing it, Babs wondered, if I got a bit tough with her? She's got to start meeting other people some time; why not now? After all, this was why Roger Mansfield had wanted her moved down to the rehab unit: so that she might start the long, slow process of getting back into the world after her horrific injuries.

Babs took her courage into both hands, remembering that it had worked when she'd half bullied, half embarrassed Colin Newbry into swimming. Perhaps she could do something similar for Liz.

'I'm going down to the hydrotherapy pool,' she said as she finished her massage. 'There's a patient there that I have to look in on this morning. If I make you comfortable here in your chair I'll manage to get back just in time to sort you out for lunch. We might even try a few more exercises if I can fit them in.'

'But you promised that you would look after me today, even though Jane's not here. She always does my other exercises before lunch. You promised, Babs.'

She looked fretful and frightened, and for a moment Babs almost gave in, but that, she knew with absolute certainty, would be wrong. If she didn't push Liz now, neither she nor Jane might be able to in the future.

'I promised that I would give you your whole range of treatment, Liz, not in what order. If you will let me help you into the wheelchair, that will count as part of your exercises. I can take you with me to the pool, and supervise my patient there, then bring you back and settle you for lunch. You can stand up and sit down a couple of times; that will count as another exercise. And you can do your breathing exercises on your way to the pool. We'll go by the outside route, but in the shade so that the hot sun won't bother you. That way you'll get plenty of fresh air.'

'But. . .' quavered Liz, her mouth beginning to tremble.

Babs said cheerfully, 'Of course, if you'd rather stay in the day-room I'll make you comfortable there until I can get back.'

'Can't I go back to the ward?'

'No, sorry, love, the ward's being cleaned, and anyway you're an up patient now, for the mornings at least; you're not allowed to skive around in bed. The doctors might decide to send you back to the main hospital if you don't take advantage of being here in the rehab unit. Look, what about putting on those new silky pyjamas that your mum brought you? The Chinese ones with the wide legs. You'll look brilliant in those and they'll cover you from neck to ankle. Nobody will see your scars.'

Liz gave in then, quite suddenly. She wasn't over the

moon about it, but at least she agreed. Perhaps she could see that Babs was determined to get her outside; perhaps she realised that she must face other people some time, and now was as good a time as any. Most likely she was afraid of returning to the main hospital with its busy wards and very sick people; she would certainly hate that.

'All right,' she said in a grumpy voice. 'I'll go to your old pool, but you'll bring me back if. . .if. . .' Her eyes filled with tears.

'If you find it too much? Of course I will, love. Whatever you may think right now, I'm not an ogre, you know.'

Liz sniffed and raised a smile. 'You could have fooled me,' she said.

The outing was a success from the start. The pale blue pyjamas that Liz's loving mum had brought in a few days before looked gorgeous, matching Liz's baby-blue eyes. The soft, high mandarin collar on the side-buttoning tunic almost completely concealed the ugly scars that ran up the left side of her neck. Liz's fair hair, which had been cut short when she first came into hospital, had grown into soft, bubbly curls, which Babs brushed until they shone in the morning sunshine.

The first person they saw when they entered the hydrotherapy pool house was Colin Newbry. He was swimming strongly from one side of the pool to the other. There was an aide in the pool with him, and, on the side of the pool, Guy, with a stop-watch in one hand and a clip-board in the other.

'That's marvellous, Colin, you've chopped off another half-second,' he called out. He looked up and saw Babs, and beamed at her. 'Am I glad to see you,' he said, sounding very excited. Babs felt the blood rush to her face. But a moment later she realised that his pleasure in seeing her was for a professional rather than a personal reason. He thrust the clip-board at her. 'Look,' he said in a low voice. He prodded the board with his pencil where he had scrawled some words.

Babs bent her head to see what he had written. She read, 'Left leg moved slightly?'

'Are you sure?' she whispered, casting a quick look at Liz to see if she was all right. It was a relief to see that she was not only all right, but absorbed in watching Colin swim backwards and forwards.

'No,' said Guy. 'That's why I'm so glad that you've come; we can check it together. In fact, if you'll take over the stop-watch, I'll go into the pool and watch what happens. But I don't want Colin or anyone else suspecting anything. It may just be a false alarm.'

'Colin,' he called, 'I'm coming in to give you a race. I'll just go and get my things off. Staff is going to time us.' He tore round the pool towards the changing-rooms, and in the space of a few seconds reappeared in striped boxer swim-shorts. Babs stared at his bronzed body in admiration; his rounded and well muscled thoracic and shoulder muscles showed off his narrow hips. Her stomach churned. She had seen him several times in swimming gear, but the sight of his athletic body never ceased to thrill her. How easy to imagine. . . No, enough of that.

He dived in from the side of the pool and lined himself up beside Colin. 'Right, Staff,' he sang out. 'We're ready when you are.'

Babs nodded. 'One, two, three, go,' she shouted, and the two men moved off smoothly through the water.

At first they remained neck and neck, then gradually Guy began to drop behind. They turned at the end of the pool and Colin, with his strong arms that supported him everywhere, began forging ahead. Of the watchers, only Babs realised that Guy was deliberately dragging behind so that he could watch Colin's legs. She knew that in spite of Colin's tremendous improvement since he had taken to swimming, further developing his shoulders and arms, Guy could almost certainly out-swim him.

But Guy had a much more important goal in mind than going all out to win. His patient, on whom he and all the staff in the rehab unit had lavished care and dedication, might just be going to prove all the experts wrong and gain the use, or part at least, of one of his legs.

Guy was focusing on Colin's left leg. It seemed at the moment as rigid as the other leg; the whole lower trunk and useless limbs were being dragged along behind the man's powerful torso. Could he have been mistaken? Babs wondered. Yes, easily from where he had been standing; with the water rippling, he might easily have imagined movement. He dropped back a little more so that his head was level with Colin's legs. No, he hadn't been wrong she thought; there it was again, a sort of hesitant twitch, very small, down the length of the left leg, causing the foot to jerk slightly outwards.

Babs made signals at him. He'd seen it too. He

looked really excited, as if he wanted to jump out of
the pool, haul Colin out and tell him. . .tell him what?
That his left leg had twitched? What would that mean
to a layman, even such an intelligent and informed
layman as Colin? He'd either dismiss it as nothing, or
imagine that he was going to walk the next day. No,
Colin must not hear anything about what had happened
until the neurosurgeons had been told. It was up to
them to decide what to do.

Babs continued to make signals at him. Catch up,
she was signalling, and he suddenly seemed to realise
how important it was that he should do so. Nothing
would alert Colin more easily to the fact that something
unusual had happened than to find him too far behind.
He put on a spurt, and within a few metres drew
abreast of his patient. Colin found some extra power,
and in seconds had touched the finishing rope, ahead
of Guy by half a metre.

There was the sound of applause from above them,
and they looked up to find both Babs and the girl in
the wheelchair clapping like mad.

'Well done, Colin,' said Babs. 'You had Dr Lloyd
beaten there all right. Congratulations.'

'Thanks.' Colin turned to look at Guy. 'What happened to you, Doc? You disappeared from view at one
point. I thought you were giving the race to me.'

'No way, old chap. I had a touch of cramp which
slowed me up for a moment.'

'Funny that should happen to you,' said Colin. 'I
thought I was going to get cramp at one point, till I
remembered that there's no way that could happen to
me, more's the pity.'

'Oh. . .' Guy strove to sound casual. 'Mine was in my right leg; where did you fancy yours was?'

'Left leg,' said Colin, without much interest. He was busy staring at Liz. 'And this is Liz Pilbeam, I reckon, the mysterious lady who keeps herself hidden away.'

'Yes, this is Elizabeth,' confirmed Babs. She knew that there had been much speculation about Liz, especially from the men's section of the ward, separated by a corridor from the women's cubicles.

Colin virtually ignored Babs. 'Did you enjoy the race?' he asked Liz eagerly.

'Oh, very much. I thought you swam very fast. Dr Lloyd had a job to keep up with you.'

Colin looked pleased. 'Why don't we sit together for lunch?' he suggested. 'Then you can tell me how great you think I am in the pool,' he finished with a laugh.

'I might just do that,' said Liz shyly. 'If Staff Nurse Babs will let me.'

'Why not?' said Babs. 'I think it's a great idea.'

It took some time with the help of the swimming aide to get Colin out of the pool, and all the time Babs was conscious of Guy suppressing his excitement over the minuscule movement in Colin's leg. Obviously the fact that Colin had felt something which he dismissed as impossible was terribly important. On this, and the combined evidence of Guy and Babs that his left leg had moved of its own volition, would depend the response from the neuro consultants. They were notoriously hard to impress, having heard so many claims that 'dead' limbs had shown signs of life. Even other doctors had a job to convince them.

When at last Colin was sitting in his wheelchair, dry

and warm, and talking animatedly to Liz, Guy suggested that an aide wheel Liz back to the terrace outside the dining-room, while Colin could trundle along under his own steam beside them.

'At last,' breathed Guy when the two patients had left. 'Now what do you think, Babs? Did Colin's leg move, or didn't it?'

'Well, I think it did — twice. Look.' She thrust the clip-board at him. 'You see, I put down the times; there's a fifty-second gap between them. Surely the powers that be will be convinced that something happened?'

'Oh, they won't doubt that; what they will doubt, probably, is if those small movements denote any real change in Colin's condition, or whether it was just some kind of involuntary spasm. The fact that both of us were there will add weight, and the fact that we both heard Colin say that he felt some sensation will be even more substantial.'

Babs could hardly contain her excitement. 'Guy, wouldn't it be wonderful if these movements prove significant? Can you imagine what a difference it will make to Colin, just to be able to hope that he might get even partial use back in one leg?'

Guy put his hands on her shoulders, and she was aware of them burning through the thin cotton of her uniform. His voice was deadly serious when he spoke. 'Babs, I feel, as you do, excited as hell about this, but it is very important that we don't let Colin have an inkling of what we suspect. It would be the cruellest blow of all if his hopes were raised and nothing came of it. You let Sister know what happened, and let her

decide if any of the other staff should be told.
Meanwhile, I'm going to get hold of somebody from
Neurology and let them take it from here.' His hands
tightened on her shoulders a fraction, and he bent
forward and brushed his lips on her forehead. 'Here's
hoping,' he said softly. 'And I'm so pleased that you
and I are in this together.'

Her heart pounded in a ridiculous fashion. He was
pleased to be with her; it didn't matter that it was for
professional reasons. 'Yes, so am I, Guy, very pleased,'
she said, striving to remain calm. 'My granny would
say that it is "a fine wee miracle".'

'My dear girl, if it comes to anything, it'll be a bloody
great miracle.'

CHAPTER FIVE

THERE was a limit to how long Colin could be kept in the dark about the possible change in his condition, even though it might be for his own protection. By the following day he had been visited by several neurological and other consultants, all of whom carried out various tests and examined and questioned him exhaustively.

Late that afternoon he was told that something extraordinary might just be happening to his left leg. No promises were made as to what might happen; everything was low-key, the news being delivered in a flat, precise voice by the senior consultant neurologist.

'You will have to undergo many more tests, Mr Newbry, and start on a programme of carefully monitored physiotherapy, and only time will tell us if there is anything like a regeneration of nervous tissue.' He didn't find it easy to put medical language into terms that a layman might understand, but he tried. He also managed a wintry smile of sorts, and patted Colin's arm sympathetically. 'It'll be a long haul.'

The fact that he was as excited as his colleagues about Colin's condition he kept well hidden. He had long ago given up believing in miracles. Only the logic of diagnosis, supported by indisputable findings, made any impression on him, but even he had to admit privately that at present this patient's case was baffling, and, medically speaking, shouldn't have happened. Well, that was a mystery that in time he would solve.

It took Guy, who had come back to the ward after escorting the great man from the unit, and Babs, who was on duty, half an hour to talk Colin down to earth. It wasn't surprising that he was on such a high, considering that for a long time he had thought that he would be totally paralysed from the waist down for good. For him, the glimmer of hope that this minuscule movement in his leg had given was like a blazing beacon.

Guy wrote him up for a sedative that night, afraid that he might be too excited to sleep and unable to cope with the situation the following day.

'I'm concerned,' he confided to Babs, his thick dark blond brows creasing together in a frown, 'that he'll come down with a hell of bump within the next few days and get depressed; you know how easily that can happen in this sort of situation. As old Logan said, it's going to be a long haul, and will need endless patience from all concerned, and most of all from Colin himself.'

'Well, it'll be up to us to prevent anything going wrong, and we will,' said Babs confidently as they returned to the office. 'And Guy, I know I said this yesterday at the pool, but I must say it again — congratulations on spotting what was happening to Colin when he was swimming. Full marks for observation, Dr Lloyd, as my old form mistress would have said.'

She sat down at the desk, ready to begin the report for the night staff. It was very quiet in the unit at this time of day. Most of the patients were in the day-room or outside taking part in various activities, supervised by staff.

Guy seated himself on the opposite side of the desk. He looked quietly pleased.

'I take that as a great compliment, coming from you,' he said. 'You're so on the ball, especially where patients are concerned. In fact you're on the ball full stop. You're full of energy and bounding with good health, like one of those before-and-after vitamin pill adverts. To use an old-fashioned word, you are always full of zest.' He gave her a quirky smile, and touched her cheek lightly with a forefinger. 'I just thought that I'd throw that in, as we seem to be exchanging professional compliments.'

Babs put her hand up to her cheek where he had touched her, and then dropped it again, hoping that he hadn't noticed. Her heart pumped madly.

'You're no sluggard when it comes to it,' she said, almost too brightly, to cover her confusion. 'Tennis, swimming, cricket. . . Whatever's on the menu, you're in there.'

He grinned. 'I like to keep active,' he said. He paused for a moment and stared out of the window. 'And I believe it's good for our patients, having staff around who know about competitive sport; after all, so many of them are young and should be leading active lives.' He looked thoughtful for a moment, and leaned his elbows on the desk and supported his chin in his hands. Babs was very conscious of his blue eyes searching her face, as if weighing her up. 'Speaking of tennis. . .' he said.

'Were we?'

'Among other things. Are you and Roger playing tonight?'

'No, he's on duty.'

'Right, well, Jane won't be playing either — she's still recovering from this tummy bug — so why don't we have a knock-up together? We'll try to find another mixed doubles pair to practise with. Are you on?'

Beneath the desk Babs clenched her hands at the pleasing prospect of spending the evening with him, without the safety-net company of Jane and Roger.

In a composed voice she said, 'That'd be lovely. Yes, I'd like that. We can't afford to miss out on practice.'

'No, we can't.' His eyes bored into hers searchingly, seeming to read her mind. 'Presumably Roger won't object?'

She was surprised that he asked; did he really think that there was something serious between her and Roger? It was possible; she had certainly used the poor man as a bit of a smoke-screen to hide her own feelings after the swimming-pool episode. She just hadn't realised that she had been so successful. She shook her head. 'No, of course not, will Jane?'

It was his turn to look surprised. 'No,' he said firmly, 'she won't; she has no reason to mind.' He leaned back in his chair, and linked his hands behind his head, stretching his legs out in front of him. He half closed his eyes, so that she could only see a glint of blue between the lids. What on earth was he thinking? 'Good,' he said softly after a moment. 'That's settled; we'll meet at the clubhouse about half-past seven.'

'Fine. I'll be there.'

'Great. That's just great.' He got up in one easy

movement. Because of the heat, he had discarded his white coat when they left the ward, and was wearing a blue striped shirt, with the sleeves rolled up. He stretched his bare bronzed forearms upwards, and the sun shining obliquely through the office window glinted on the fair hairs that sprang along the flexed muscles. He smiled down at her; his blue eyes, enhanced by the blue shirt, gleamed enigmatically. He knows, she thought, that I'm imagining his arms round me, holding me so tight that I can hardly breathe.

She let out a sigh, and lowered her eyes quickly. He bent forward, leaning on the desk, his arms even closer, his lean, healthy muscles like whipcord, glinting gold.

His voice, when he spoke, was deeper than usual, and husky. 'I'm looking forward to this evening,' he said, 'I hope you are, Babs.' Their eyes met again for a moment. 'Let's hope we can find another doubles pair; I should like very much to play as your partner for once, instead of your opponent. It should be quite an experience.'

'Yes,' she said, pleased with her even voice, 'we can suss out each other's game from the inside, as it were.'

He nodded. 'Exactly,' he said with a knowing smile. He straightened up and made for the door, opening it wide. 'Bye for now,' he said softly. 'Be seeing you.' And he was gone, leaving the office achingly empty.

She heard his footsteps receding down the corridor. 'Bye, my darling,' she whispered.

She hadn't meant to say that; it had just slipped out. It was ridiculous. What would he have thought had he heard? Would he have minded that involuntary endearment? She didn't know; he gave so little away, in spite of the almost intimate conversation they had just had, in spite of the invitation to play tennis. Best not to read anything into that. She mustn't over-react. She must accept that he was something of an enigma, and leave it at that. She hadn't known what had stopped him kissing her that day by the pool, or why he had turned away from her, and she still didn't know what made him tick where his personal feelings were concerned, even after all these weeks. All that she really knew about him was that he was a brilliant and ambitious doctor, and a pleasant and sociable companion. How deep his feelings went for anything outside work she had no idea. Nothing in his attitude when they met off duty conveyed anything more than a light-hearted approach to relaxation. And that included his attitude to Jane.

Well, at least there was no doubt about his enthusiasm for tonight's tennis practice. He was definitely keen about that and had shown it. Now she must put him out of her mind while she was on duty, and concentrate on work.

Stop daydreaming, she told herself; just buckle down.

Once off duty, and changing into her tennis gear, it was much more difficult to keep her mind from daydreaming and anticipating the pleasure of being in Guy's company for the evening.

She reminded herself that it wasn't the first time she would share an evening's tennis with him; she and Roger had played against him and Jane frequently. It had been relatively easy when the four of them were together to accept Guy as just another player and keep things in perspective. There had been nothing intimate about it. Tonight was going to be quite different. Guy would be on her side of the net, and they would be playing together against a common opponent. She tried to rid herself of the idea that there was something symbolic about the two of them playing together. How stupid can you get? she asked herself in disgust as she savagely stuffed her jazzy cotton shirt into the waistband of her shorts.

She arrived at the clubhouse before Guy, and ordered an orange juice. 'I'd better save the stimulating stuff till later and keep a clear head,' she said to Tina, who was serving behind the bar. 'Win or lose.'

'Who are you playing with tonight?' Tina asked.

'Dr Lloyd, if we can find a pair to play against.'

'Well, you'll be all right, then,' said the barmaid. 'He's a smashing player, isn't he? I think he's lovely, absolutely brilliant.'

'Yes, he is nice,' said Babs inadequately, squashing her desire to enthuse over him.

She took her drink out to the terrace. There were a couple of empty chairs at a table where Gemma Long, the red-headed staff nurse who had befriended her on her first day, was sitting. She was absorbed in conversation with a young man whom Babs didn't recognise.

Babs made her way over to the table. 'May I?' she asked.

Gemma flashed laughing green eyes at her. 'Sure and why not? Let me introduce you to Bill Marks, new junior reg on Paediatrics. Bill, this is Babs Becker-Brown; she staffs on Rehab.'

He and Babs shook hands as she sat down. 'Are you two playing?' she asked.

'We're booked for the next free court. Should be coming up soon,' said Gemma. 'I suppose you and Roger are playing as usual.'

'Roger's on duty, but Guy's joining me for a game, as Jane's still off with this tummy bug thing.'

'Shall we make it a doubles match?' asked Bill. 'That's if you wouldn't mind, Gemma.'

'Fine by me, but I should tell you that both Babs and Guy are top-notch players. I don't know what you're like, Bill, but I'm what you might call an erratic player — pretty awful sometimes, and worse than awful at others.' She beamed at them both cheerfully. 'But if you want to risk it. . .'

'Let's risk it,' said Bill. 'If Babs is game.'

Babs nodded. 'Great,' she said. She had the feeling that Bill would have risked anything to spend the evening with Gemma.

At that moment Guy arrived on the terrace. Babs caught her breath with pleasure at the sight of him. He looked incredibly fit and athletic in a kingfisher-blue knit shirt, and brief white shorts that showed off his long muscular legs to perfection.

He was looking round for her. She raised a hand, which he acknowledged as he weaved his way round the tables and chairs.

'Hi,' he said. 'Sorry I'm late.' He placed a warm, firm hand on her shoulder, and looked into her eyes, and her heart gave a great bound of pleasure as she realised that he was soundlessly telling her how pleased he was to see her. She let herself respond to his touch with the faintest of tremors.

This time she wasn't imagining anything; his eyes spoke volumes.

Her cheeks flushed a dusky rose under her pale tan.

'Doesn't matter,' she said softly. 'You're here now, and I've been talking to Gemma and Bill.' She patted the empty chair beside her, and Guy slid on to it, pulling it closer to her chair as he sat down. It was an effort to talk; she wanted to sit there and soak up the look and feel of him. He was so close that she could feel the heat of his body, smell his cologne. It was intoxicating.

She took in a couple of ragged breaths and dragged herself back to reality. 'Have you met Bill?' she asked brightly. 'He's just started on Paediatrics.'

'Yes, we've been introduced.' The two men nodded amiably to each other, and then Guy greeted Gemma, and grinned at Bill. 'I see you haven't wasted any time finding our Gem of a staff nurse to show you around.'

'Would you believe she offered?' said Bill. 'I couldn't believe my luck, but then, like the good nurse that she is, she spotted my masculine charms immediately.'

'Well, naturally,' said Guy with a laugh, looking straight at Babs. 'Actually, nurses find us medical chaps irresistible.'

'Men!' said Gemma with a grin.

'Doctors!' said Babs, smiling into Guy's eyes.

We're flirting, she thought happily, and he doesn't seem to mind, and the setting couldn't be more perfect.

It was a beautiful summer's evening, with the still hot sun burning in a cloudless blue sky and bathing the courts in golden light. To Babs, sitting beside Guy, revelling in his nearness and his obvious pleasure in her company, the sound of balls on rackets and cheerful voices echoing in the clear air added to her euphoria. It was romantic, and as near perfect as one could get.

The conversation buzzed around her, and she automatically said the right thing, and laughed in the right places, but for her the only reality was Guy sitting beside her, his leg pressed against hers so that she could feel the downy hairs on his calf softly chafing her bare leg. From time to time their eyes met, and she felt herself drowning in their blue depths, spiralling down and down, holding her breath till it hurt and she had to come up for air and force herself to look away from him to break the spell.

She was conscious all the while that life was just going on around them as if nothing special was happening. With a jolt she realised that it might just be happening to her, and not to Guy; perhaps he was untouched by their eye contact, and was not left breathless with desire as she was. She stole a sideways glance at his face as he was talking across the table to Bill. He seemed to sense that she was looking at him and even what she was thinking, for he took hold of her hand and squeezed it gently. He knows, she thought with relief, and he feels the same. Her heart thumped in her chest, and she felt dizzy with delight.

At that moment a court became available and they went off to play a rather zany game until a dusky twilight settled over the net, and the ball kept disappearing in the fading light. Gemma had spoken the truth about her playing—it was grotty compared to that of the other three—but it didn't matter. Nobody minded one bit. Babs and Guy simply excelled themselves, returning impossible and miss-hit balls, and Gemma's Irish charm made fun of it all, reminding them that it was just a game, a transient thing.

They made their way to the clubhouse when they could no longer play in the purple twilight, and they were invited to join a crowd at one of the large centre tables. There was a squash of bodies and chairs, and Babs and Guy ended up thigh pressed to thigh, arm to arm.

Babs shivered. 'Cold?' asked Guy softly, his voice nearly lost in the surrounding din of other voices.

'No, happy,' replied Babs, her eyes glowing, not caring if she was giving herself away.

'But you're shivering.'

'Not because I'm cold,' said Babs, darting him a questioning look from beneath her long lashes. His brilliant blue eyes looked darker than usual; his mouth twitched slightly at one corner. His face was very close to hers.

His voice dropped an octave. 'Then why are you shivering?' he asked, and there was a hint of gentle amusement in his voice.

'Because. . .' He's teasing me, she thought. She wanted to say, Because you are close, because you are touching me, and sending shock-waves through my system that I can't do anything about. But of course she didn't. Even with all that had happened she couldn't bring herself to be that bold. She was still a little uncertain of what his reaction would be to such a statement. 'Oh, I expect someone is walking over my grave,' she said with a smile.

She could see that he didn't believe her. 'Ah,' he said. 'Is that what it is?' His leg pressed harder against hers as his eyes searched her face. He put out a hand and tucked a tendril of her short tawny hair behind her ear. Her heart, which had already taken a beating that evening, thumped painfully as his finger touched her skin, and she was sure that he must sense it.

This is humiliating, she thought; I'm behaving like a schoolgirl. I must get a hold on myself, and say something to break the spell. I'm going to make a fool of myself if I don't. Before she could think of anything either silly or intelligent to say, Tina the barmaid's voice rang out over the babble of conversation.

'Dr Lloyd,' she was calling, 'can you come to the phone, please. There's someone wanting to speak to you.'

Guy uttered an oath under his breath, and scraped his chair back from the table. 'Sorry about this, love,' he said as he looked down at Babs. He raised one eyebrow. 'What timing.'

Babs tried not to show her mixture of disappointment and relief at the interruption. She shrugged. 'Goes with the job,' she said.

'Well, officially I'm not on call,' said Guy. 'I can't think who it is.'

He moved away round the crowded tables. The roar of voices started up again. But I can, thought Babs, and some strange sixth sense told her that it was Jane White.

Babs sixth sense had been right.

'That,' said Guy, when he returned to the table ten minutes later, 'was Jane.' His face was impassive, but she thought that anger, or something like it, lay just beneath the calm exterior. 'She hopes to be well enough to work tomorrow.'

'Oh, good,' said Babs, unable to think of anything else to say, and wondering why Jane had thought it necessary to let Guy know at this time of night. And what else, she wondered, had they talked about for ten minutes? Had Jane been checking up on Guy? It was a possibility. Though Guy had made it abundantly clear that she had no rights to do so. Perhaps she didn't feel the same.

Lying in bed later that night, trying to will sleep to come, Babs wondered how the evening would have ended had Jane not made that phone call. Would the earlier magic have worked some miracle for her and Guy, and brought them together? Or would the spectre of Jane have made that impossible? For though Guy had been quite adamant about his relationship with Jane having no bearing on what he did, her phone call had certainly spoilt the intimacy of the evening.

Soon after he returned from taking the call he had escorted Babs back to the nurses' home and wished her a very cool goodnight. After a moment's hesitation he had kissed her cheek in a casual fashion, and with that meaningless gesture wiped out all the warmth and unspoken declarations of feeling that had been passing between them all the evening. They might just as well not have happened, she thought miserably. At the end of what had started as an evening of magic, she was left feeling empty and betrayed. The fact that she hadn't been a hundred per cent sure how she wanted matters to develop with Guy was very little comfort. She would have liked to make that decision for herself, and not have it forced upon her by Guy's sudden coolness.

On this unhappy and unsatisfactory note, she eventually fell asleep.

Work the next day was not the panacea to pain or distress that it usually was. She couldn't at first drag her thoughts away from Guy, and the delights of the evening that might have been. As Sister Crewe was on a day off, Babs was filling in for her. This meant that she had to read and discuss with the day staff the report, and decide what action to take on each patient. After going through the patients one by one, Babs dispatched the nursing staff about their business attending certain people. She herself decided to have a word with Colin Newbry.

Colin, in spite of his sedation, had had a restless night, alternately dreaming and waking, wishing that he could walk again. He was full of questions, reasonably wanting to know about his future treatment and the possible prognosis arising out of the previous day's tremendous news.

Babs could not tell him more than he already knew, which had been fully explained to him, but Colin wasn't satisfied. In spite of the restrained explanatory remarks made by Dr Logan, the neurologist, today he wanted more definite evidence of his condition, and found it

hard to believe that there was not more to be discovered at present than had been told to him.

Babs stood by his bedside and repeated what the
night staff had told him *ad nauseam*. 'Colin, you know
as much as I or anyone else knows at this moment.
You're a complete puzzle to everyone, including the
eggheads in Neurology. Even they have not come
across a case quite like yours.'

'Is that really true? Nobody's trying to keep anything
from me?'

Babs drew in a deep breath, determined to be
patient, and prepared herself to repeat what she had
just said all over again.

'I can assure you that what Staff has told you is the
truth, Colin,' said Guy's deep, firm voice from behind
Babs. 'So let's have no more nonsense about it. Can't
have you badgering my nursing staff to death.'

Neither Babs nor her patient had heard him enter
the cubicle. He was standing at the foot of the bed. He
looked tired and remote, unlike his usual cheerful self,
though he produced a smile for Colin. Babs was so
pleased to see him that she wanted to thank him for
coming to her rescue and give him a hug, but, as that
was impossible, offered him tea instead.

'I'm just going to make some fresh in the office,' she
said. 'Come and have a cup.' She turned to her patient
and said in a no-nonsense voice, 'You're OK now,
aren't you, Colin, now that Dr Lloyd and I have both
reassured you?'

Colin gave them a sheepish smile. 'Yes, thanks, I'm
fine. Go on, go and get a cuppa; you both look as if
you could do with it.'

Back in the office, Babs made tea, glad to have something constructive to do with her hands. 'Sister's off,' she explained. 'So I'm acting up, and have all this at my command.' She waved a hand round the small office. She felt the need to be facetious and remove, if she could, the stern look from Guy's face. 'Colin gave the night staff a right run around, and got quite stroppy, insisting on seeing Sister Crewe, or whoever was in charge; that's why I was in with him so early. I'm glad you came along when you did; I didn't know whether I was going to be able to reassure him on my own.'

She spoke quickly and nervously, trying hard not to show how much his presence affected her. It seemed especially important after their unsatisfactory parting last night.

Guy took a swig of tea, and looked speculatively at Babs, as if assessing her state of mind. 'About last night,' he said. 'Jane's phone call. . . I'll explain.' He seemed detached, almost indifferent, as if the matter was almost a bore.

'There's no need,' said Babs in a rush. 'We were only having a game of tennis, for heaven's sake; I'm happy to confirm that to Jane.' She squashed memories of their silent exchanges, of his thigh being pressed against hers, and his willingness to drop his guard and flirt outrageously with her.

A strange expression flitted across his face for a moment. His eyes were steely blue. 'I don't need anyone to vouch for me,' he said with an austere dignity. 'Jane doesn't own me. What I do with my spare time is my own affair. Please remember that.'

She compressed her lips, and in a hard little voice said, 'Sorry if I offended you, Guy; nothing was further from my mind.'

He said in an icily calm voice, 'Offended? I'm not offended, just disappointed that you should think that I need defending, or that I did, said or implied anything outside my control yesterday evening. I am a free agent; I thought that I'd made that clear.'

Babs had never seen him like this before — angry in a restrained, whiplash sort of fashion, as if he was coiled ready to spring at something, or someone. This was a Guy whom she didn't know.

She didn't know how to respond, but it didn't matter. There was a perfunctory knock on the door, which was opened before she could answer, and Jane entered. She stood in the doorway, looking pale, presumably from the aftermath of her tummy upset. Her smile was bright, but her eyes glittered strangely as she looked at Babs.

'Hello, darling,' she said to Guy, radiating warmth towards him. 'I thought I'd find you in here, but with Sister, not with Babs.' Her glittering eyes held the steely look that Babs had seen once before, soon after she had arrived at Princes. Then it had been so fleeting that she thought that she had been mistaken, but there was no doubt now about that look: it was one of intense dislike.

It was, as it had been for weeks, a hot morning, yet Babs felt suddenly chilly and shivered as goose-pimples and tiny hairs on her arms and at the back of her neck raised themselves. She actually blinked under Jane's malevolent gaze, and felt the need to swallow as if she had a lump in her throat.

'Sister's day off,' she said in a calm enough voice, as if nothing had happened.

Jane's eyes lost their unpleasant expression immediately. Her face cleared. 'Oh,' she said, sounding relieved. 'You're acting up?'

'Yes.'

'Oh.' She looked across at Guy, who had turned to look out of the window. 'You'll be wanting to get on with sorting patients out. Sorry I interrupted.' She smiled at Babs, a normal nice smile, and at Guy's unyielding back.

Guy turned abruptly, spinning on his heel, so that the rubber squealed on the polished floor. 'It's all right, Jane.' His voice was very even, expressionless, and the smile that he gave her seemed to Babs to be false, superficial, though it seemed to please Jane. She beamed at him. He went on briskly, 'Babs and I have finished our business.' He included Babs this time in a wintry smile. 'See you later, ladies.' He nodded at them both as he strode towards the office door, and left.

A silence fell on the office for a moment after Guy had left. Babs was almost afraid to meet Jane's eyes, lest she saw a repeat of the bitter dislike that had been revealed in them earlier, but she made herself do so, smiling pleasantly at the same time.

'You seem to have got over your bug all right,' she said. 'Though I must say you still look a bit pale.'

'Well, I threw up a lot, and had diarrhoea,' Jane replied, pulling a face. 'I suppose it's not surprising really if I look washed out, but I feel fine, and couldn't wait to get back to work.' She smiled nicely at Babs. 'Now, Acting Sister, who do you want me to start on first, and is there anything new to tell me about anyone?'

It was disconcerting speaking to a normal Jane after the earlier episode, when if looks could kill Babs would surely have dropped dead on the spot. This was the Jane she knew and liked, who loved her work, was a clever and sensitive physiotherapist, and who was fun to work with. The difference between the two Janes was strange, to say the least, but it existed, and for the moment it was Babs's job to latch on to the good physio.

The two of them spent a short while going over the treatment book, with Babs filling Jane in on the stupendous developments connected with Colin Newbry. It was decided that Jane should start work on Liz Pilbeam, managing on her own, as Babs had previously done, until she needed help, then Babs would give a hand in between doing Sister's work.

'I've got a feeling that Liz fell for our Colin,' she told Jane, 'when I first took her to the pool. Even with all the excitement connected with Colin I noticed how she reacted to him, and she was only too ready to go out again yesterday and return to the dining-room for lunch.'

'Golly, that's a huge improvement in her emotional reaction.'

'Isn't it just? We're all thrilled with her and for her.'

'My word,' said Jane, with a rather rueful look on her face. 'It doesn't do to be away for long in this place, does it? Too many things happen as soon as one's back is turned.'

For one moment Babs thought that Jane was referring to matters on the personal front, and her heart thumped madly with something like fear, but Jane's eyes when she met them were quite normal, their usual, bright hazel-green, kindly and compassionate.

She let out a sigh of relief, and said cheerfully, 'Well, that's Rehab for you — a hive of activity at all times.'

'You can say that again,' said Jane, and she went off to attend to Liz Pilbeam, leaving Babs, a little dazed, to concentrate on her paperwork.

CHAPTER SIX

THE following days passed busily, and Babs was grateful for the constant activity in spite of the heat. Her thin uniform dress stuck to her uncomfortably as she went from patient to patient, and she spent as much off duty time as possible in the cool, silky water of the pool. In the back of her mind she hoped that she might meet up with Guy when she was swimming, but strangely she never did, though there were always plenty of other staff enjoying the refreshing cool of a swim. Was he, she wondered, deliberately avoiding her, except for tennis practice?

It was now late July and the evenings were beginning to show signs of drawing in, with dusk descending nearer nine o'clock than ten. She and Roger, and Guy and Jane, continued their practice matches. They were, with other members in the Princes Park club, preparing for the finals, to be held in August.

On the surface nothing seemed changed; the four of them were good friends.

Babs's feelings about this were ambivalent. She couldn't make up her mind whether she was relieved or not when Guy made no attempt to speak to her privately. His dealings with her when on duty were friendly, but entirely professional. There was nothing about his manner to suggest how close they had come on the night that they had played tennis together, and for this she was, in a strange way, grateful. She told herself that she didn't want to become entangled with anyone, not even this enigmatic, exciting man who made her heart bump and her senses reel when he was near. Her career was all that mattered.

Resolutely she struggled to put behind her those shadowy thoughts of love that had beset her for the last few weeks. Guy Lloyd, she told herself, was just a good friend, and she would not give in to what her silly heart and mind was saying to her. Anyway, she had no evidence at all that Guy felt strongly about her, except for their silent exchanges and his gentle teasing on that one magic evening, and of course the earlier frustrating incident by the pool. But a little flirtation was not enough, she told herself sternly, to prove that a sophisticated man like Guy was in love with her.

As if to confirm that this was a sensible resolution, one morning, in a burst of confidence, Jane told Babs that she and Guy were virtually engaged. Babs knew then that, whatever her feelings for Guy, she must squash them. He apparently didn't consider himself attached to Jane, but she thought otherwise.

Babs was quite shattered by what Jane had to say about her relationship with Guy. 'We've known each other since we were children,' she said. 'And we were always expected to marry.'

'And what do you think, Jane? Do you want to marry Guy, or is it just because it was expected of you?' That was a hopeful stab in the dark; perhaps there was the dimmest chance that Jane wanted to marry Guy because of other people's expectations rather than her own.

'Good heavens, no. I've always wanted to marry him, ever since we were kids together.' She seemed genuinely surprised at being asked.

Babs felt mean, ferreting for information, but she just had to know.

'And what about Guy; does he feel the same?'

'Oh, absolutely, though he sometimes talks about his work as being an obstacle, and he has warned me that it will be a long time before we can marry. He wants to get his consultancy first.'

It shouldn't have mattered, but Babs was for some reason relieved to hear that Guy was being cautious, though it surprised her too. He was sensual and masculine, and didn't seem the sort of man prepared to wait to possess the woman he loved. Well, that didn't necessarily mean marriage, but, as far as she knew, Jane lived a blameless, sex-free life in a shared house in the village, and Guy lived in bachelor quarters here at Princes.

She shook herself out of her reverie. 'But it may take years,' she said. 'Won't you mind waiting that long?'

'Oh, not a bit,' said Jane happily. 'I'll wait forever if necessary.'

Babs had no answer to that, though she thought that forever was a bit over the top. She wouldn't have the patience to wait that long if she were in love. She felt strangely sorry for Jane, but didn't really know why. After all, she was the girl with whom Guy was supposed to be in love, the girl who seemed to be able to twist him round her little finger, however adamant he was about not being romantically involved with her.

Swallowing the sadness which seemed to be lying beneath the surface of her life these days, she concentrated on work when on duty, and enjoyed Roger's continuing cool friendship when off duty. He began to be important to her, and, though at times she felt guilty for using him to assuage her unhappiness on account of Guy, she was able to squash this emotion in the knowledge that she enjoyed his company and he enjoyed hers.

Ten days after Jane had dropped her bombshell about her relationship with Guy he came into the office when Babs was again relieving Sister Crewe. Sister had taken an extra day off suddenly, in order to visit a sick relative, and her absence took Guy by surprise.

He knocked at the partly opened door, entered, and had even begun to say, 'Sister. . .' before he realised that it was Babs and not Sister who was sitting at the desk.

'Oh, it's you, Babs,' he said in mild surprise. 'I was looking for Sister.'

Babs felt her heart lurch, something that she believed she had now got under control, managing when they met on the unit or the tennis court to suppress such reactions. But then she usually had time to prepare herself, and there were other people present. His sudden appearance threw her. Being alone with Guy within the confines of the small office was something she hadn't bargained for. She got herself in hand and presented a friendly but professional front, struggling to ignore the effect on her senses as the faint but sharp scent of his cologne reached her and his sheer male magnetism threatened to engulf her. He seemed to fill the small office with his presence.

'Yes, it's me, Guy.' She managed a bright smile. 'Sister had to take an extra day off for personal reasons.'

Guy looked at her thoughtfully. He brushed his hand over his head in the familiar gesture that she found so intriguing, and raised one eyebrow in what she took to be amusement.

'So you're in charge,' he said. 'Little Babs Becker-Brown, queen of all she surveys.' His eyes travelled over her, examining her from head to foot in an almost arrogant yet at the same time teasing manner.

Babs flushed to the roots of her hair, and thrust a report slip into his hand.

'I expect you want to know about the new patient,' she said. 'The chap with the motor neurone condition. He's only thirty-eight; that's young, isn't it, to be already showing symptoms?' she babbled on mindlessly. Since Guy had assessed Basil Norton for admission to the unit, he obviously knew all about him. But she had to do something to quieten her still raging heartbeats, and divert Guy's too personal attention. She didn't think that she could handle that.

Guy grinned, and she knew that he had seen through her. He pushed the paper back across the desk.

'No, I didn't want to see Sister about Basil; he's not due to be transferred for a couple of days. It's about Colin Newbry and Liz Pilbeam.'

This came as a surprise to Babs, enough to shake her out of her preoccupation with her reactions to Guy. Her concern now was wholly for her patients.

'Surely,' she said, 'within the limits of what we still know about Colin's extraordinary improvement he's doing very well? Nobody expected him to do more than he is to start with; the muscle tone in his leg is still poor after so long being unused.' She was quite indignant at the thought that anybody expected more from Colin, who was working so hard at his physio. 'As for Liz, she's in a marvellous frame of mind these days, since she and Colin became friendly. She's really prepared at last for plastic surgery, and is less conscious of her scarring than she's ever been.'

'Oh, yes, physically they're both on the up; no one would quarrel with that. Your defence of them does you credit.' He looked at her with a humorous gleam in his eyes. 'Look, I'll tell all; just rustle up a cup of coffee, black with sugar. I need a boost.' But, for all his joking manner, his mood was serious as he sat down and crossed his long legs and looked rather grimly out of the window, his well formed lips set in a straight line, his bleached fair hair glowing like a halo round his head in the sunlight filtering through the blinds. He had never looked more handsome, or more unobtainable, to Babs. He seemed so contained, so self-sufficient, right out of her reach. How could she ever have imagined. . .?

She caught her breath. 'Yes, of course,' she said. 'I'll make coffee.' At least she could do that to please him. She plugged the kettle in to boil. Since Guy still didn't seem inclined to say more, but sat staring thoughtfully at his hands, she asked, 'Have I missed something to do with Colin and Liz? I've been off for a couple of days.'

Guy lifted his head and looked straight at her with speculative blue eyes, and an ironic curl to his lips. 'Yes, you have, haven't you? You've been missed, my dear Babs, in every sense.'

Her pulses raced, and her skin prickled; she hardly dared look at him. What did he mean — that he missed her on duty, or personally, emotionally, physically? She met his eyes. The expression in them was no longer speculative, but glowing, warm, intimate, inviting; it was as if he were touching her in spite of the space between them. She felt as if she were melting under his gaze; it seemed deathly quiet in the office.

She put a hand on the desk to steady herself, and said, her voice seeming to come from a long way off, pleading, 'No, Guy, you mustn't look at me like that.' She blinked back tears. 'It's not fair. What about Jane?'

Guy let out an explosive oath. 'Jane?' he said. 'What the hell's Jane got to do with us?'

Babs said through gritted teeth, 'I know all there is to know about you and Jane; she's told me. Now please, Guy, let me make your coffee and talk patients.' She snatched the kettle from the narrow shelf, and splashed boiling water into the two mugs, and over her left hand. 'Oh, damn, damn, damn,' she said fiercely, slamming the kettle down and staring at her scalded hand. 'What a fool I am.'

'In here,' said Guy, jumping up and dragging her into Sister's tiny cloakroom. He turned the cold tap on and held her hand beneath the rushing water. 'Keep it there,' he said sharply. 'You silly girl, what the hell do you think you're playing at, being so clumsy?'

The tears that she had been trying to keep back

started to roll down her cheeks. 'D-don't shout at me, please. I didn't do it on purpose. It was because you . . .you. . .' Words failed her; tears streamed down her face.

Through her tears she saw the angry expression on his face soften and change to one of compassion and gentleness. He said in a low voice, 'Babs, my dear girl, why the tears? Of course you didn't do it on purpose.' Keeping one hand over the wrist of her scalded hand, lying limp beneath the gushing water, Guy put his other hand under her chin and tilted her head up so that her brown eyes were looking directly into his blue ones. In the confines of the tiny cloakroom they stood close together. There was no need for words. Babs knew that he was going to kiss her, and she knew that she couldn't resist him.

He took his hand from her chin, and used his fingers to smooth the tears from her face. 'You poor darling,' he whispered in a low, throbbing voice. 'You lovely girl; I'm mad for you. I want to make love to you; you know that, don't you?' His eyes were dark and luminous.

Babs nodded. 'Yes,' she whispered.

'And you want to make love to me?'

'Oh, yes,' she breathed.

Her thumping heart threatened to choke her. She swallowed, lifted her free hand, and ran it over the stubble of his hair. It was soft and silky, not spiky as she thought that it might be. She pulled his head down, down closer to her own. 'Kiss me,' she begged, 'please.'

'Not really the time or place,' he murmured, 'but what the hell?' His warm breath fanned her face as his lips came down to meet hers in the beginnings of a kiss.

They locked together, straining against each other, noses rubbing noses, and gently nuzzling each other. Guy let go of her scalded hand, and with both his hands stroked and caressed the contours of her face and neck, and cupped her small breasts, rubbing his thumbs over her nipples straining erect against the thin material of her dress. One hand trailed down her back and smoothed her hips with gentle, sensual movements, pressing her against his body, hard with desire. Her legs almost gave way, and only his muscular arms supported her as she swayed helplessly against him.

It was Babs who first became aware that someone was tapping on the office door. With a little moan she struggled to free her lips from Guy's. 'Door,' she mumbled. 'Someone's at the door.'

With calm, deliberate movements Guy eased himself away from her. He gave her a wolfish grin, and his eyes gleamed with savage humour. 'We'll finish this business another time,' he said softly. 'And don't forget I want you, my darling girl.' His eyes challenged her for a moment, daring her to disagree with him, but Babs merely nodded, unable to think clearly, still in a mild state of shock.

He took her scalded hand, lying limply beneath the cascading water, and called out, 'Come in,' in the coolest of voices.

The door to the office opened, and a timid voice, which Babs recognised as belonging to a first-year student, asked, 'Staff, will you come and have a look at Mrs Smith, please?'

Before Babs could reply Guy called, 'Please come in here, Nurse; we need your help.'

The young nurse walked through the office and appeared in the cloakroom doorway. Both her eyes and her mouth formed an Oh, and she squeaked as she stared at Babs's hand being held firmly beneath the tap by Dr Lloyd. 'Staff, you've hurt yourself.'

'Yes, I stupidly spilt some boiling water over my hand. It was a good job that Dr Lloyd was here to rescue me.' And if he hadn't been here, she thought, it would never have happened.

'Nurse,' said Guy, at his most charming and authoritative, 'go to the fridge in the treatment-room, and bring me ice, wrapped in gauze, and a bandage. Then explain to the patient that Staff or I will be along to see her shortly. OK, can you do that?'

'Oh, yes, Doctor, of course. PDQ.' She returned Guy's smile and sped away to do his bidding.

They had a few moments before she would return with the ice pack that Guy had ordered.

Babs tidied herself with her one free hand, straightening her uniform, tucking strands of her short tawny hair beneath her cap. She knew that she must preserve her image in front of the staff, for her own sake, and Guy's. She couldn't believe that she had been so abandoned here in Sister's cloakroom. She blushed furiously, and met Guy's teasing look.

He seemed unperturbed by what had happened; in fact his eyes were alight with humour, even as he straightened his tie and ran an unnecessary hand over his short hair.

Relax with **FOUR FREE** Romances plus two **FREE** gifts

Whatever the weather a Mills & Boon Romance provides an escape to relaxation and enjoyment. And as a special introductory offer we'll send you FOUR FREE Romances plus our cuddly teddy and a mystery gift when you complete and return this card. We'll also reserve you a subscription to our Reader Service which means you could go on to enjoy :

◆ **SIX BRAND NEW ROMANCES** sent direct to your door each month.

◆ **NO EXTRA CHARGES** free postage and packing.

◆ **OUR FREE MONTHLY NEWSLETTER** packed with competitions (with prizes such as televisions and free subscriptions), exclusive offers, horoscopes and much more.

◆ **HELPFUL FRIENDLY SERVICE** from our Customer Care team on 081-684-2141.

> **Turn over to claim your FREE Romances, FREE cuddly teddy and mystery gift.**

Free Books and Gifts claim

Yes Please send me four Mills & Boon Romances, a cuddly teddy and mystery gift, absolutely FREE and without obligation. Please also reserve me a subscription to your Reader Service; which means that I can look forward to six brand new Romances for just £11.40 each month. Postage and packing are FREE along with all the benefits described overleaf. I understand that I may cancel or suspend my subscription at any time. However, if I decide not to subscribe I will write to you within 10 days. Any FREE books and gifts will remain mine to keep. I am over 18 years of age.

2A4R

cuddly teddy   mystery gift

Ms/Mrs/Miss/Mr _____

Address _____

_____

_____ Postcode _____

Signature _____

Reader Service
FREEPOST
P.O. Box 236
Croydon
Surrey CR9 9EL

Send NO money now

Babs said with as much calm as she could muster, 'I don't think she noticed anything, do you?'

Guy shrugged. 'No, I'm sure she didn't. Probably thinks we're too old for any such nonsense. Now how's the hand?' He lifted it clear of the water and examined it closely.

'The ice pack idea was brilliant,' said Babs.

'Not really; the proper drill for a minor scald.'

'But you thought of it. My mind had gone blank at that moment. I couldn't think of anything.'

He laughed out loud. 'At times,' he said, 'you are almost as naïve as that girl. You blush like a schoolgirl; it's delightful.' His eyes swept admiringly over her.

'Don't,' she pleaded. 'Don't look at me like that. I. . . I——'

She got no further, as the office door burst open and Jane appeared, followed by the student nurse.

'Are you all right, Babs?' Jane asked. 'I hear that you've scalded your hand. Is it very bad? We've brought ice with us.' She seemed to see Guy for the first time. 'Oh, what a blessing you were here, Guy, to make sure that Babs kept her hand under cold water.'

'Yes,' drawled Guy, 'wasn't it?' He grinned at Babs, who looked away hastily.

'Well,' said Jane impatiently, 'what does it look like now? Has the inflammation gone down? Has it blistered?'

Guy turned off the tap, and gently patted Babs's hand dry with a towel before he examined it. 'No, no blistering,' he said. 'But still inflamed. Let's put on the ice pack.' He held out his hand, and Jane handed him the crushed ice bagged in gauze. Guy placed it carefully over the back of Babs's hand, spreading it so that it tucked itself into the crease between her thumb and palm, where the redness was most pronounced. Carefully he wound the bandage in a figure-of-eight round her hand, securing the ice pack. He finished round her wrist. 'There,' he said, 'that should do it. Now put on a glove, and you should be able to carry on as usual. I'll have a look at it later this evening.' His eyes met hers. 'About six,' he suggested impersonally. 'In the treatment-room.'

The rest of the day for Babs passed with a dream-like quality. Nothing seemed quite real. For once she wasn't able to contain her exuberant thoughts beneath a cloak of professionalism; they were too chaotic and intoxicating for that. Again and again she found herself re-living those intimate moments with Guy, and blushed with pleasure at the memory of his hands exploring her body, and exciting her in a way that no one had before. The fact that it had happened in the down-to-earth surroundings of the office added a peculiar piquancy to the situation.

Work went smoothly enough; it was routine, and her injured hand made little difference to her ability to do various jobs. Jane remained a pain, being over-helpful, unknowingly making Babs feel guilty. But, guilty or not, Babs still thrilled with excitement at the memory of what had passed between herself and Guy. It had seemed so right, so natural, that she felt it couldn't be wrong.

All the doubts about Guy's integrity that she'd been unhappily hugging to herself for the past weeks began to dissolve as the day wore on. She didn't have any more concrete information than she'd had before concerning the true situation between him and Jane, but she was now absolutely sure that Guy was innocent of any real deception. Whatever Jane had said, Guy didn't behave like a man with a guilty secret, at least where she was concerned; quite the opposite, in fact. Jane's name, even vaguely suggested in the context of a loving relationship, infuriated him. She knew, without a doubt, that the man who had kissed with such tenderness and passion this morning would simply not be involved with another woman. He wouldn't allow himself to be; he had too much pride.

He said that he wanted to make love to me, she reminded herself, and was adamant that there was nothing between him and Jane. But could she be sure? And those last words that he had uttered — 'I want you' — were they significant? Shouldn't he have said instead, I love you? And another thing, she reminded herself; if Jane wasn't a problem for Guy, why had he behaved so strangely that day by the pool, and why, if he loved her, had he let weeks go by without seeking her out to tell her so? What other secret was he hiding?

Babs sighed; it was no good tormenting herself. She had no answers, but nothing could take away from her the wonder of his kisses and caresses this morning, and the certainty that she loved him. There was probably a simple explanation for everything, and this evening when they met they would talk it through. The idea of talking, doing something constructive, even if it was only exchanging ideas, quite restored her optimism and her marvellous feeling of happiness, of being loved and

wanted. Life was wonderful. She was convinced that
tonight they would between them resolve any problems
that faced them.

Love, she decided, was powerful enough to do that.
Roll on this evening, and her meeting with Guy. He
was a strong, sophisticated man who knew exactly what
he wanted out of life, and wouldn't let anything stand
in his way. His compassion for his patients made him
an even stronger doctor. He was a man to be admired
and loved, and, surely, trusted.

CHAPTER SEVEN

IN FACT fate intervened, and she didn't see Guy at six o'clock that evening, or alone and socially for the next few days.

At four-fifteen the whole hospital was put on alert. There had been a horrific train crash at the local station. The emergency crash team went into action, and every available ambulance was drafted to Park station.

While they were waiting for casualties to arrive the background to the crash filtered through. A train carrying local schoolchildren had been rammed by a fast train that should have been diverted round the station on another line. Instead, it had passed through the station at high speed, and ploughed into the local train, shunting it forward and derailing it, and only coming to a halt when it concertinaed and reared up on to the platform.

The numbers of killed and injured were not yet known, only that there were many of them.

Sister Crewe, who had been off duty, reported back the moment she heard the news. Together with Babs and another staff nurse she organised the day and treatment block of the unit for use as an overflow from Casualty. Rehab was ideal for this. It had rooms available that were not in constant use, and it was in an excellent position for ambulances to approach direct

101

from the drive, or from the casualty block, via a minor drive.

The job of the Rehab staff was to make comfortable and hold casualties until they could be assessed and sent elsewhere. Minor injuries could be dealt with on the spot; more serious ones were re-routed through Casualty or theatres to the wards. Most of the assessing was done by housemen, while Guy and other registrars assisted in theatres and A & E.

Casualties started to arrive at about five o'clock, and continued to be ferried in during the evening.

Sister Crewe sent Babs back to the office just after they had dealt with the latest influx of bleeding and shattered passengers.

'We're going to have a long night, Staff,' she said grimly. 'You go through to the office and do the normal report and reassure everyone. We mustn't forget that many of our patients are still traumatised by accidents in the recent past, and might be affected by this.'

She was quite right; it took some time to settle everyone and hand over to the night staff.

It was half-past nine when she finished and made her way back to the day-rooms full of casualties.

She relieved Sister Crewe, who went off to have something to eat.

'You can go when I get back,' said Sister.

She was looking dreadfully weary after an already traumatic day spent visiting a very sick relative in another hospital. In fact she had only just arrived back at Princes when the alert began, and had gone straight on duty, stopping only to change into uniform. She was obviously loath to leave the casualties even for a short while, but experience would warn her that she must have something to eat and drink, to enable her to carry on for what might be a long night. 'I'll be about twenty minutes,' she told Babs. 'And then you can get a break.'

Babs looked with concern at the older woman. 'Make it half an hour,' she said, giving her senior a dimpling smile. 'I promise I won't let anything happen while you're gone. Go, Sister, there's plenty of us here; we'll manage.'

'All right,' agreed Sister thankfully, returning Babs's smile. 'Half an hour, then it's your turn.'

It was just after ten when Babs made her way to the Rehab dining-room, which had been turned into a running buffet for helpers and relatives of victims. Along with other parts of the hospital, it, and the staff, had switched over to an emergency situation, as had been planned, smoothly and efficiently.

Sympathetic domestic staff were dishing out hot drinks and sandwiches. It was quite heart-warming how people pulled together in a crisis, Babs thought as she wearily bit into a cheese sandwich and swallowed a mouthful of soup. She closed her eyes for a moment and leaned against the wall, and wondered what Guy was doing.

'Babs,' said his voice in her ear. 'Are you all right, love?'

Her eyes flew open. Weary as she was, it thrilled her to hear his voice. 'I'm fine, what about you?'

'In hospital parlance, as well as might be expected,' he replied, with a rather crooked smile. 'It's because it's kids, of course; it makes the senseless carnage seem so much worse. Well, as long as you're OK. . .' He gave her arm a reassuring pat. 'I'll go and forage for food; I've got twenty minutes before I'm back in Theatre.'

In spite of his smile, Babs could see that he was tired; there were lines on his smooth, tanned face that hadn't been there before, especially around his eyes and mouth. She guessed that he was as much emotionally drained as physically.

She shoved the remains of her soup and sandwich into his hand. 'Have this; I'll go and grab more.'

'Thanks; can you rustle up some black coffee with tons of sugar?' He gave her another lop-sided smile, and his blue eyes gleamed with humour for a moment. 'Nice to have a personal slave at my command.' He examined her face carefully. 'You're sure you're all right, Babs? You must be up to your eyes in it on Rehab, being used as an overflow for Casualty.' He leaned forward and brushed her cheek gently with his lips. 'Try not to let the kids get to you; it's too painful. One's just got to press on regardless.' He pulled a face. 'And not get involved.'

Babs was surprised and comforted by his kiss, and by his words. What a wonderful doctor he is, she thought, so caring, and he must care for me too, to consider my feelings. 'Thank you,' she whispered, touching her cheek where he had kissed her. 'That'll keep me going. Now I must go and grab that food.'

She went away to collect coffee and more sand-wiches, and when she returned she found him sitting on the floor, hunched against the wall in a small space between two window embrasures.

'Shortage of chairs,' he said. 'God, what a crowd in here.'

Babs crouched down beside him. He looked hot. There were sweat marks on the thin white T-shirt that he had been wearing beneath his Theatre greens, making it stick to his chest and ribs. All the windows were wide open on to the still, dark night, but the room was stifling, airless, like an oven.

The room was packed with staff snatching a snack, as she and Guy were doing, and with strangers too, relatives of victims of the crash, waiting for news of their loved ones. A couple of social workers moved about among them, gathering information, offering comfort, and police officers were doing the same.

Tired as she was, she could appreciate the magnitude of the task that the hospital had to undertake, not only to provide medical attention for the injured, but also to keep track of patients, identify them, and link them up with anxious relatives. It was a miracle that everything seemed to be under some sort of control, an ordered chaos. Clearly the practice runs of 'Operation Adrenalin' had been successful, if such a word could be applied to this appalling situation.

Guy was eating automatically, with his eyes closed, but he sensed Babs looking at him, and opened them, giving her a cloudy blue, rather surprised look.

He smiled wryly. 'Dear God,' he said. 'I nearly dropped off. No stamina; that's my problem. I'm glad I didn't opt for surgery; all those hours standing — not my scene at all. I'd much rather be doing a marathon.'

He gave a dry laugh. 'But I dare say I'll survive.' Already his eyes were brighter, his voice firmer. A few minutes' rest and sustenance had been all that he needed to restore him to his usual fit and able self.

'I don't doubt it,' said Babs. She too was feeling much better for her break, and also for seeing Guy; he had cheered and reassured her. She stood up and smoothed out the creases in her uniform, then bent and felt bold enough to drop a kiss on his forehead.

He caught at her hand; it was the bandaged one. 'Good lord,' he said. 'I'd forgotten about your burn. How is it?'

'Fine, and I'd forgotten about it too. Who wouldn't, with all this going on?' She indicated the milling throng of people. 'What's a small burn?'

'Depends on who's burnt,' he said. He turned her hand over and dropped a kiss on the soft inner part of her arm, and she shuddered with pleasure at the touch of his lips. 'Take care,' he added softly, 'and that's an order.'

'Yes, sir,' said Babs, bobbing a little curtsy. She didn't want to leave his strong, safe presence. She turned away. 'Goodbye, Guy,' she said abruptly.

It was some days before Princes Park returned to anything like normal, and even then the rehab unit was still using day cubicles for in-patients, who had been transferred from acute wards to make beds available for casualties.

The four patients—three men and one woman—were pleased to be in the more free and easy atmosphere of Rehab, especially knowing that this meant they were on their way home.

On the third morning following the accident Babs and Jane started work with Basil Norton, the motor neurone patient, who was the first warded patient to have been moved, since he was already on the list for rehab treatment.

There wasn't a lot that could be done for him, but, in these early days of his condition having been diagnosed, it was important to offer every assistance, and help him maintain his dignity and self-help for as long as possible. He had accepted his condition courageously, and for a layman had known quite a bit about it.

'I know,' he'd said, 'that this wretched thing is ongoing, and that the most I can hope for is perhaps an occasional remission. I'm grateful that I'm likely to keep my marbles, and can go on thinking, and, though I know that speech can go early on, I'm hopeful that I won't lose it for quite a while yet. That's important to me, as I'm a writer, and I must be able to use my tongue or my hands to get anything on paper.' He smiled engagingly. 'If I can do that, I can keep going, and so will Sophie. I'm just glad that we haven't got kids.'

'Sophie? Your wife?' Jane had asked.

'Live-in companion, lover, girlfriend, call her what you will. She's marvellous; we've been together for years. She used to be my secretary; now we co-author a lot of stuff, and as long as we can go on doing that. . .' He had stopped talking then, lifted his chin, and smiled again, this time defiantly. 'If we can carry on writing together,' he said, 'we'll cope with this situation.'

Sophie, when she came to see him, agreed whole-heartedly. 'As long as he can go on writing,' she said, 'he'll get by.'

'And you?' Babs asked. 'Will you get by?'

'Yes,' said Sophie. 'But I wish there'd been a baby. That would have made us complete.'

'Surely it's not too late,' said Babs, 'if you think you can cope with a baby and a sick man.'

'Basil seems to think that it's a good thing that we haven't got a child,' said Sophie. 'I don't think he'd agree to our trying for one now.'

'Then it's up to you to convince him otherwise,' said Babs firmly. 'If you feel strongly about it. After all, you're both in this as a team, and it's important that you both feel as happy and satisfied as possible to cope with what's ahead of you. Perhaps it's not a good idea to think of having a baby in your situation, but who can tell? Look, there's a leaflet about counselling on all aspects of MND; I'll go and get you one from the office. There's bound to be someone qualified to give help and advice.'

Thinking of babies and being in love made her think of Guy. For a moment she let herself picture a future with Guy, and being married to him, with a houseful of small children with blond hair and startling blue eyes. But she squashed the thought. It was ridiculous to link her feelings for him, and a relationship that hadn't even got off the ground properly, with anything as serious as babies. He certainly wouldn't be interested. He was a careers man through and through;

hadn't he made that clear to Jane? And on her own account she wasn't ready to settle down to a life of domesticity, so there was no point in indulging in such thoughts.

She was concentrating on sifting through the folder of leaflets that held all manner of information about the many conditions they treated on the unit when Guy suddenly spoke to her from the office doorway.

She hadn't seen anything of him since that traumatic evening of the accident. He had briefly visited the rehab unit between working flat out in Theatre, but never, as it happened, when she was around.

'Playing at being Sister again, Babs?' he asked, with a laugh in his voice.

Babs promptly dropped the sheaf of papers she was holding, and they slipped and slithered all over the floor.

'Sister and the senior physio are at a management meeting,' she said breathlessly, feeling the blood rush to her cheeks with the sheer delight of seeing him. He was dressed in shorts, a sleeveless vest and running shoes. She teased in a voice imitating Sister Crewe, 'Coming to do a casual round, Doctor? Or is this the new uniform for registrars?'

Guy gave a crack of laughter, and Babs thought that she had never heard anything so joyful in her life. It almost wiped away the weeks of doubt, which had been partially laid to rest when he had kissed her in Sister's cloakroom. He looked, except for a few tired lines round his eyes, as he had on the day when she had first met him: a commanding, slightly arrogant, but at the same time charismatic figure.

Of course, it couldn't really be quite like that any more. It was impossible to put the clock back, and too much had happened in their emotional response to each other for nothing to have changed, but it was wonderful to catch a glimpse of the early Guy.

She made a great effort to be cool and professional. 'Did you want Sister?' she asked. 'Or somebody else?'

He grinned wickedly, and his eyes twinkled suggestively. 'I want you,' he said. 'No one else.' Then he added, suddenly serious, 'Babs, it's time we talked, really talked, and dispelled some of this nonsense that you've got in your head. We need to pick up from where we left off the other day when you scalded yourself. That was for real, and we both know it, and we know too that we fancy each other like mad, don't we?'

They were crouching down among the scattered papers. He leaned against the side of the desk, and looked at her through half-closed eyes. His bronzed arms were folded over his chest, his strong, muscular legs half doubled beneath him as he squatted on his heels, and the long blond silky hairs on his thighs glistened in the hot sunbeams that slanted between the slats of the window blinds.

Babs caught her breath. He had never looked more masculine, more dominating. He radiated strength and charisma. His half-closed eyes held her spellbound. She longed to feel his arms about her, to feel his superbly fit body pressed against hers. What had he said? Something about fancying each other and needing to talk?

'Yes,' she said, letting out a sigh. 'We do. Need to

talk, I mean,' she added hastily, not meaning him to imagine that she was agreeing with him about anything else.

He smiled, another of those wolfish, knowing smiles. 'Good girl,' he said, and reached out and patted her hand. She snatched it away from him, trying to ignore the electrifying effect his touch had on her. He simply smiled more broadly at this gesture, as if he understood exactly the effect he was having on her. 'Right, let's arrange something.'

'All right, when and where? I was due to meet Roger tonight for a practice match, but I could cancel, I suppose.' She tried to sound casual.

'Then cancel Roger. Unless a practice match is more important than us.' He raised a mocking eyebrow.

Babs shook her head. 'Of course not,' she muttered, 'but what about Jane? Aren't you seeing her tonight?'

'Jane?' Both eyebrows shot up. 'What has Jane got to do with me taking you out for a meal and a chat?' He didn't wait for a reply. 'But it so happens that she's meeting friends tonight, if that makes you any happier.'

'Oh, yes, of course, I remember, in Guildford — physios who trained with her.'

'That's right.' He shrugged. 'A reunion or some such nonsense.' He sounded very dismissive. 'I'll pick you up at seven-thirty outside the nurses' home.'

'Is that wise?' she asked. 'Someone's bound to see us, and inevitably it will get back to Jane. You know what this place is for gossip.'

'My dear girl, you seem to be obsessed by Jane. For goodness' sake, leave her to me. If there's any explaining to do, I'll do it.' He gave an exasperated sigh, and then leaned forward and planted a kiss on her surprised mouth, which left her wide-eyed and trembling. 'And that,' he said, 'is to be going on with — a first instalment. Now be good; I'm off jogging.' He shoved the leaflets that he had gathered into her hands, and left.

She had a last view of his white trainers as he disappeared into the corridor, and she was still grubbing round for the remaining leaflets when Sister returned from her meeting.

'Can I help, Nurse?' she asked good-naturedly as she entered her office.

'No, it's all right, Sister, thank you. I've finished, and I've found the leaflet I wanted for Basil Norton's friend, about MND. I must take it to her before she leaves.'

'Then don't let me stop you,' said Sister.

Babs was waiting outside the nurses' home when Guy drew up in his classic MG. Since she had no idea where he might be taking her for their tête-à-tête, she had dressed in a short, silky, creamy white shift dress with an important-looking wide suede buckled belt slung low on her slender hips. She draped a rainbow-striped, light wool stole round her shoulders, and slipped on poppy-red, low-heeled strappy sandals, with a shoulder-bag to match. Her freshly washed tawny hair gleamed with vigorous brushing. She was groomed to go anywhere, she felt, a plush French restaurant or a country pub.

She also felt that her cool, sophisticated outfit complemented the serious side of her meeting with Guy. If they were to have an in-depth conversation about their future, as he had intimated, she would at least be dressed for the part.

Guy gave her a wolf-whistle as he leapt out of the car, swept the door open with a flourish, and guided her into the passenger seat.

Babs giggled. 'Am I going to get this gentlemanly treatment for the rest of the evening?' she asked sweetly.

'Madam, I'm always a gentleman,' he said gravely, as he bowed over her hand. His eyes were full of admiration, but there lurked in their depths an expression that told her that he was conscious that tonight's meeting was not to be taken lightly.

Like her, he had dressed with care, and was wearing lightweight grey trousers, a tunic-type white collarless shirt and a pale blue jacket. A pair of grey leather shoes completed his outfit. He too was dressed to go anywhere, sophisticated or casual, Babs realised.

'I've booked a table at a pub-cum-hotel in Portsmouth,' he said as they started down the drive. 'It's rather charming; it overlooks the harbour, where there's always plenty of activity, with small boats and the bigger naval ones from the dockyard. It'll take us nearly an hour to get there, but I promise you it will be worth it.'

'Sounds lovely,' said Babs, injecting a false enthusiasm into her voice, suddenly realising that she was nervous. She wondered if Guy was feeling less cool and collected than he appeared to be. After all, this wasn't just a jolly night out, but an occasion for explanations. He probably wasn't looking forward to that part of it, even though he seemed so in control.

From the way he dismissed all references to Jane, she didn't seem to be a problem where he was concerned, but Babs couldn't forget the expression that had lit up Jane's face when she spoke of Guy. And anyway, even if the Jane business was satisfactorily resolved it didn't mean that all was plain sailing for them. No way had she anticipated, when she took up her post at Princes Park, an affair that would interfere with her career. It was still her goal to remain at Princes and learn all that she could about rehabilitation nursing before moving to a more senior post up north or in Scotland. Nothing was going to stop her doing that.

Guy would feel the same about his work, she acknowledged silently, as she replied monosyllabically to his comments about the countryside that they were speeding through. His ambition to become a consultant specialising in rehabilitation medicine was as strong as ever. Nothing would stop him achieving his ambition. Love and marriage might be all right for some people, but not for her, not for Guy; they were both career-orientated. All that was left was a relationship of sorts, and she was by no means sure that she would find that acceptable, even if offered. 'We fancy each other', he'd said. True, she thought, but it's not enough, not for me.

She wished with all her heart that she had not fallen in love with him; life would have been simpler that way. She could see only problems ahead, and all for nothing, or just a short-term, passionate interlude before their work took them on separate paths.

It didn't bear thinking about. She looked sideways

at Guy, her heart leaping into her throat as she examined his handsome profile. He was quiet too; perhaps he was having second thoughts about this evening and their planned discussion. In spite of the warm summer evening sunshine, she shivered and pulled the rainbow stole closer round her bare shoulders.

Guy quickly turned his head. 'Cold?' he asked.

'No, scared,' she said, taken unawares and unable to prevaricate.

'Scared?' He was surprised. 'Whatever are you scared about?'

'Whatever we talk about, I suppose. Us. . . Jane. . . It doesn't come easily, does it, planning to hurt someone, even when you know that it's got to be done?'

'Babs, I don't know what you're talking about.' He turned his head again sharply.

Babs felt dreadful. She was handling this badly. She had started out in such a mood of optimism; what had happened to it? It seemed to have evaporated, and had left her feeling wretched. She loved Guy, but did she love him enough to consider changing her career plans if they clashed with his? She couldn't bring herself to say, as Jane had said, that she'd wait for him forever. That surely was love, and meant that Jane loved him more than she. But did that give Jane more rights?

They were both silent for a few more minutes, then Guy said, all sharpness gone, 'We'll be there soon.' He took a hand from the wheel and patted her hands lying limply in her lap. 'It's going to be all right, Babs, I promise you. What we need to do is talk. We can resolve any problems.'

'Yes,' said Babs, trying to smile. 'I expect you're right.'

He pulled in to a cobbled car park behind the old inn, which stood on the harbour walls. In spite of being depressed by her thoughts in the car, Babs exclaimed with delight as she looked out over the busy waters of Portsmouth harbour, alive with boats and ships going about their business. The nearly setting sun, gleaming orange-red on the water, added to the beauty of the scene.

'That's the Isle of Wight,' said Guy, pointing south across the water to where a large hump dominated the horizon. 'Have you ever been there?'

'No.' Babs shook her head.

'Lovely island; all sorts of scenery packed into a small space. You can get round it in a day. Hilly interior, sandy beaches, and cliffs, some of which are striated with marvellous colours, like your shawl.' He traced the line of her stole where it lay draped round her shoulders, and let his hand stay there, gently squeezing the top of her arm.

'You sound like a travel brochure — "Come and visit our magical island, drenched in constant sunshine",' said Babs, having some difficulty keeping her voice steady, very conscious of his arm resting along her back, and his fingers, which he had slipped beneath her stole, kneading the soft flesh of her shoulder.

'I'll take you there one day, my darling,' he said, his voice low and husky. He bent his head and nuzzled the back of her neck, oblivious of other people standing like themselves, looking out over the sun-bronzed water of the harbour. 'Babs,' he said in his velvet-soft voice, 'I want you.'

'And I want you,' she replied in a whisper, trembling at his touch. Her very bones seemed to shiver as his fingers moved sensuously up and down her arm. She wanted to melt against him, into him, be wrapped around by him.

He must have read her thoughts. He moved behind her and dropped his hands round her waist, pulling her against him so that she could feel how much he longed for her. 'God,' he muttered into her shining tawny hair. 'You're lovely, utterly desirable.'

'I'm glad you think so,' she whispered back, and felt his arms tighten around her, and his hands caress her hips.

They stood there for a long time, watching the red-hot sun sliding towards the watery horizon, and lights on the island pricking out through the warm purple dusk.

'Darling, we must go in,' Guy said at last, breathing unsteadily, 'or we'll lose our table.'

'Yes.' She turned in his arms, and lifted her face to be kissed. To her surprise, he kissed her gently, without passion, as if aware that now he had mentioned the mundane matter of eating the real business of the evening had begun. She swallowed her disappointment. He was right, of course; they had come here to talk.

She shivered, and this time, she told herself, it was partly because the setting of the sun had left the dusky night chilly. She didn't want to admit that it had anything to do with what Guy might divulge.

She disengaged herself from his arms, and he let her

go without protest. 'Goodness, it must be getting late,'
she said, with only the slightest hint of unsteadiness in
her voice. 'No wonder I'm starving. Come on, beat you
there.' She turned away from him and ran across the
cobbled yard to where light streamed out from the
back door of the inn.

Guy caught her up, and took her hand, and together
they walked into the lamp-lit, aromatic dining-room of
the Buccaneer.

CHAPTER EIGHT

THE first person Babs and Guy saw as they entered the restaurant was Jane. She was sitting at a table with several other women, laughing and talking.

Babs stopped dead in her tracks, and Guy, a little behind her as they followed the waiter to their table, came to an abrupt halt too.

'I don't believe this,' said Babs, turning to Guy. 'Wasn't she going to Guildford or somewhere like that for this reunion?'

'Indeed she was,' said Guy, an exasperated note in his voice. 'Trust Jane to be in the wrong place at the wrong time.'

'Well, I don't suppose she arranged to be here because of us; she couldn't know we were going to turn up,' Babs said, in as light a tone as she could manage, and trying to squash a rising tide of panic.

'Want to bet?' replied Guy, with a dry, humourless laugh. 'It's all part of Jane's witchery, or sixth sense, or whatever, where I'm concerned. We don't seem to be able to avoid each other. It's been like that since forever.'

The waiter had arrived at a table set for two, not far from where Jane was sitting. He was looking round, smiling at them, as he pulled out a chair. 'Madam,' he said to Babs. She slid into the proffered chair. 'Sir.' He pulled out the other chair.

'Thanks,' said Guy, but he didn't sit down. 'There's a friend of ours at another table. I'll have a word. Leave the menu, please.' He seemed, now that his spurt of anger had subsided, rather amused by the situation. Babs wished that she could emulate his calm; she felt uncomfortably churned up inside.

'Sir.' The waiter left the menus, inclined his head, and went away.

Jane had not seen them arrive, so engrossed was she in conversation with her companions. For one treacherous moment, as, heart in mouth, Babs watched Guy approach the other table, she wished that they had disappeared while they had the chance. After all, Jane would not then be hurt by the knowledge that her 'fiancé' was spending the evening with her close friend and colleague.

Guy had reached Jane's side; he was talking to her. She was smiling, and waving a hand, indicating that Babs should join them. Guy said something more, and then crossed back to Babs, followed by half a dozen pairs of eyes as Jane and her companions watched his progress.

'I suggested that we join Jane and her friends at their table, as there's room, and they seem only too pleased.' He smiled down at her and pulled a humorous face. 'It makes sense, Babs, trust me. Much better than sitting here trying to ignore each other's presence. I told Jane that we simply decided to spend the evening together and have a good jaw about life, the universe and all that, instead of playing tennis.'

'And she bought it?' Babs asked incredulously.

'She did, because, if you think about it, it's true,

isn't it? And what's so wrong with friends and colleagues doing just that?' He took her arm. 'Come on,
Babs, let's take this in our stride. After all, it's not the
end of the world. We can talk another time. Come and
be your usual uncomplicated and happy self.'

To her surprise, Jane greeted her with enthusiasm,
and introduced her to the group of physios as her friend
and partner at work. She apparently found Guy's
explanation for their being together in the pub far from
Princes perfectly acceptable, and didn't even question
Babs further about it. She was just Jane at her nicest.
Perhaps because she was convinced that Babs and
Roger had a thing going between them, she felt that
Babs wasn't a threat.

Some two hours later the supper party came to an
end, and, although it had not been the ordeal that Babs
had experienced, she was relieved when it was all over.
It had been the sort of get-together that in any other
circumstances she would have enjoyed, with bright,
intelligent conversation and friendly arguments about
patient care taking up a good deal of the evening. As
always, it was impossible for a group of medical
professionals to get away from talking shop.

Babs and Guy said their goodbyes and drove away,
leaving the heat and the dust of the town behind them,
beneath a black velvet sky studded with glittering stars.

They were both silent at first, privately digesting the
events of the evening, until Guy said in a neutral sort
of voice, 'How annoying that one of those silly girls
hurt her foot and couldn't drive, so they had to descend
on that particular pub for the evening.'

'Do you know how she did it?' asked Babs. She felt

almost cheerful now that the evening was over. 'I heard her saying something about it, but didn't hear the details.'

'Believe it or not, it got jammed under a hoist that she was instructing someone to use. Talk about hoist on one's own petard. She mashed up some tarsals and metatarsals, and sprained her ankle. Ludicrous, isn't it?' His mouth quirked into a half-smile at the thought. 'Apparently she was the star of this get-together, as she's off to Australia shortly to work. So it was a farewell do. She couldn't drive, so they all went to her.'

'Poor thing; what rotten luck.' Babs would have liked to keep the conversation going in this lighter vein, but her mind was a blank. She glanced sideways at Guy as they sped along, but couldn't make out anything from the expression on his face in the dim light. It was difficult to tell how much the unexpected meeting with Jane had disturbed him, for, apart from his initial spurt of anger, he seemed unruffled by the experience.

They were well out into the country when Guy spoke again. 'Pity our tête-à-tête didn't come off tonight, Babs.' He lifted a hand from the steering-wheel and patted her leg. 'But we'll sort something out in the near future, and until then, my love, you'll just have to trust me.'

His touch stirred her for a moment, but she was too busy with her thoughts of Jane and her easy acceptance of them being together to be as much affected as usual. She tried to put her thoughts into words.

'What I can't understand,' she said pensively, looking sideways at Guy to see his reaction, 'is why Jane was so — placid, I think is the word, about you and me turning up in a strange pub together, when in the past she has been so possessive about you.'

'What's to understand?' replied Guy, with a shrug. 'After all, it's not such an outlandish idea for colleagues to have a meal together. When Jane is in a rational mood she will accept that such things can happen.'

He sounded almost uninterested. Babs turned her head and peered closely at him.

He glanced at her at the same time, and shrugged again. 'That's just Jane, you see,' he said in a still expressionless voice. 'I repeat that you'll just have to trust me where she's concerned.'

A little *frisson* of anger shot through her. Why should she blindly trust Guy? Why not accept Jane's version of the situation between them? Because you want to believe him, she answered herself; because you're in love with him.

'Is that what you were going to tell me if the evening had gone according to plan, Guy, that I must take you on blind trust?'

They were in a country lane with a wide verge and fields on either side. He pulled on to the grass in front of a farm gate, and stopped. The night air was sultry, humid, hardly moving; thunder clouds had begun to roll over the horizon, although stars still shone above them.

Guy undid his seatbelt, switched on the interior light, and turned a bland face towards her.

'Babs,' he said, 'I'm damned if I'm going to take you

home until I've said what I planned to say, and you must listen with an open mind.'

The blandness had gone. Now he looked rather forbidding, his well shaped lips set in a thin line, his eyes commanding and very blue.

Babs gave a little shiver of apprehension as she turned to face him.

He took her hands in his. 'Babs, try to relax,' he said. 'What I have to tell you may be difficult for you to appreciate, but please try to understand, and don't go off in a huff.'

Tension made Babs laugh jerkily. 'I won't guarantee not to blow my top, but I can assure you that I won't go anywhere in a huff. Where on earth would I go to?'

Guy followed her gaze as she examined the warm, throbbing countryside, bathed under the light of a rising moon. It was empty apart from themselves and a few cows on the other side of the hedge.

'Good,' he said, with a laugh. 'You are what one might call a captive audience. Well, that's to my advantage.'

Babs felt better after he had laughed so spontaneously. He sounded natural, more like his usual self. 'Right,' she said with a smile. 'I'm all ears.'

Guy dropped her hands and turned to face the windscreen, leaning forward and draping his arms over the steering-wheel.

'You want to know about Jane,' he said. 'Well, we go back a long way. We lived next door to each other when we were children. Our parents were great friends. Her father was a dental surgeon, both my parents GPs, so we had quite a lot in common. Mrs White had studied to be a physiotherapist, but gave it up to marry Jane's father. That's why Jane wanted to be a physio, but, unlike her mother, she was determined to finish the course.'

'And she did.'

'Yes, though I think it was hard for her. I often wondered if her heart was in it, or she just wanted to prove something after her parents died.'

'Her parents are dead? She didn't tell me that.'

'Yes, and they died horribly in a fire. They both smoked, and when the house caught fire it was thought to be caused by a smouldering cigarette. Jane had been out that evening and came home to find smoke pouring out of the house. She came to us for help. By the time my parents did what they could and the fire engines arrived it was too late; her parents were overcome by fumes and died.'

'How dreadful. Poor Jane.'

'Poor Jane. She felt particularly bad because she'd had a typical teenage quarrel with her parents before going out. She felt that, had she been there, it wouldn't have happened. Nonsense, of course, but she couldn't be shaken from the idea. It made her quite ill for a while.'

'She had a breakdown of some sort?'

'You've guessed it, Babs, though I can't tell you more. Whatever I say will seem like a betrayal of a promise.'

'A promise? I don't understand; surely there's nothing to be ashamed of in having a breakdown?'

'No, there isn't, but some people — and Jane's one of them — feel guilty about it. Hers was a pretty bad breakdown, and I promised that I wouldn't discuss it with anyone. Do you understand?'

'Not really. That is, I can understand your having to stick to a promise, but after all this time, and Jane's professional training, it seems sad that she needs to be so secretive about it.'

'Well, let's leave it at that, shall we? Suffice to say that after the fire Jane moved in with us, and became part of the family.'

'The family? Have you brothers and sisters?'

'Two of each, but all older than me.'

'Which made Jane rather special to you.'

'Clever girl. That's exactly right. For the first time I had someone younger than me to boss around when I was home from school. I was seventeen, Jane fifteen, so I was an ideal age to feel important, to enjoy being looked up to and hero-worshipped.'

'And Jane fell in love with you and stayed in love with you.'

'Yes, unfortunately, end of story, except to say that Jane's affection for me is based on gratitude, nothing else, not a firm basis for love, marriage or a relationship.'

'You don't love Jane?'

'I'm not *in love* with her, but I do love her. Big difference,' he said laconically.

'But Jane doesn't realise this?'

'Apparently not, though I have tried to put it to her on several occasions. Eventually she will understand, when someone, or something, becomes more important. Until then. . .' He broke off, reluctant to say more.

There was a heavy silence between them, like the brooding hot summer air, scarcely moving around them. A cow mooed mournfully in the field behind the hedge, making her jump. Guy pressed her hands briefly, reassuringly.

'It's only a cow,' he said, his voice firm, strong, comforting. Babs, who had been staring out at the moonlit landscape with unseeing eyes, was startled into turning to look at him. 'Don't worry about it; don't worry about anything,' he went on. 'It's going to be all right; everything's going to be fine. I'll sort it all out, though it may take a little time. All you need to do is to be patient and trust me, Babs.'

His certainty was both reassuring and infuriating. She wanted to ask him why she should blindly trust him, but couldn't find the right words; it seemed almost petty to question him. In some ways it was a relief not to, to allow Guy to take matters into his capable hands. He was not just the pleasant friend she had grown to know and love, nor the dedicated, sometimes frustrated doctor whom she admired, but a tough, positive man too. He was arrogant at times, but she could forgive his arrogance.

'Of course.' She raised a smile. 'You will go easy with Jane, won't you, Guy?'

He shrugged. 'Naturally. I'm not a monster, my dear. Now that's enough about the matter; leave it with me.' He stretched out a hand and stroked her cheek, and then slipped his finger beneath her chin, and tilted her face to meet his. He leaned over and kissed her gently on the lips.

'There,' he said. 'Almost a platonic kiss with which

to finish this rather strange evening, but anything more at the moment would seem excessive.'

'Yes,' she said simply, 'you're right.' She found that she was glad that he hadn't been more insistent, though part of her had wanted to be wrapped in his arms and held against his taut, demanding body, and swamped with passionate kisses. As usual, he seemed to do exactly the right thing at the right time.

He started fastening his seatbelt. 'Now,' he said, 'are you ready to be off?'

Babs nodded and fastened her own belt. 'I'm ready,' she said, thinking of all the possibilities that the evening's events had opened up. 'For anything.'

Without explanation, he seemed to understand what she meant. 'Splendid.' He turned the ignition key, and let out the clutch. 'Back to Princes,' he said with a small enigmatic smile. 'And a new beginning.'

An hour later Babs lay in bed thinking about the evening, and Guy's cool toughness and self-assurance. He seemed to have everything under control.

She stared into the summer-scented, airless darkness. In spite of the reasonable, almost sensible way the evening had ended, she felt bewildered, uncertain of herself and the future, although she had said that she was ready for anything. Guy had almost seemed to enjoy the unexpected dinner party with Jane and her friends, once he had got over his initial annoyance. She still found it strange that Jane had so readily accepted Guy's explanation for their being together.

Anyway, he had told her not to worry, he would take care of things, and for once in her independent life she was glad to lean on someone, especially as that someone was Guy. She sat up and turned over her hot pillow, and eventually drifted off into a deep, sound sleep, comforted by the thought of Guy's strength and confidence.

CHAPTER NINE

To HER surprise, considering all that had happened, Babs slept well. The moment that she opened her eyes, however, the events of the evening came flooding back, as detailed as a video recording.

She could see vividly Guy's face when he had picked her up at the beginning of the evening, his nicely shaped mouth moulded into a broad smile, his eyes full of admiration; so different from his expression several hours later when they had talked in the car. Then he had been deadly serious, cool, calm and determined to sort out any problems in his own time and in his own fashion, and absolutely certain that he would succeed.

Her thoughts swirled around as she got ready to go on duty. Guy's confidence had rubbed off on her, and she felt a wave of optimism sweep over her as she went to have her shower. She knew without a doubt that he would fix everything as he had promised.

She had just come out of the shower when somebody banged on her door, and said that she was wanted on the phone.

Guy, she thought immediately, and, slipping her feet into towelling mules, she hurried out into the corridor with her towel tucked round her like a sarong.

In anticipation of hearing his voice, her respirations were coming and going rapidly, and she was quite out of breath when she reached the phone.

'Hello,' she murmured breathlessly, huskily, into the mouthpiece.

'Morning; have you just come in from a jog?' said Roger's voice in her ear. 'Because if you have, you're sadly out of condition.'

'Oh, Roger.' Disappointment at it not being Guy hit her like a sledge-hammer. She actually gasped as if she had been hurt.

'Are you all right?' he asked sharply.

She found something like her normal voice. 'I'm fine, thanks. I've just come out of the shower and I stubbed my toe.'

'Then you're even more out of condition if running from your room to the phone makes you sound as if you're about to expire. You need a good work-out; so what about our practice match tonight? Is it on, or might you have to call it off?'

'No, of course I won't; it'll be fine tonight. I'm sorry about opting out last night.'

'Think nothing of it, as long as it's OK for tonight. Let's make it a long, hard session, starting, say, at six. I'm off tonight, and, blessed relief, not even on call. What do you say, Babs? Shall we do a marathon, and really stretch ourselves?'

She'd have promised him almost anything to assuage the guilt that she felt for ditching him the previous night without explanation. He hadn't even questioned her about it, just accepted that she couldn't play, which for some reason made it worse that she had let him down.

'Let's do just that,' she agreed, meaning to, and

sounding eager. 'I feel like a really hard, tough game. Let's get out there and beat the hell out of someone.'

'If it's only each other,' said Roger in his drawling, rather sarcastic voice. 'See you at six, then.'

'See you,' said Babs.

She put down the phone and went thoughtfully back to her room. For some reason she had the feeling that Roger knew that she had been out with Guy last night; why, she wasn't sure. He hadn't said anything, or even hinted at how she might have spent the evening.

Of course, he might well have heard through the grapevine that she had been seen getting into Guy's car. So what? She was a free agent. They had no commitment whatsoever to each other, except as friends.

It was a pity, though, that she'd cried off last night without offering any explanation, just saying that she didn't want to play. Roger, being Roger, hadn't pressed her for reasons, simply accepting that she had a right to do so if she wished. It was extraordinary that he seemed incurious about other people, except where his work was concerned. Of course, it could be the fact that he was not much interested in other people, even herself, that made him almost indifferent. She'd heard him described as a cold fish, and, though she knew that this was not entirely true, he certainly projected a coldness that was, for instance, quite the opposite to Guy's outgoing friendliness.

She finished dressing, had a quick breakfast, and went on duty. The best thing she could do at the moment was to lose herself in work, and put Guy and last night out of her mind.

This wasn't difficult, as they were frantically busy on the warded part of the unit, and in addition had a large number of patients in for day treatment. There were injections to be given, dressings to change, and other purely nursing jobs that had increased since the extra patients from the main hospital wards had been admitted to make room for the train victims.

She was just about to get stuck into this long list of jobs when Sister Crewe asked her to wait after giving the night report to the staff.

'I want to talk to you about Colin and Liz,' she said. 'I would have done it days ago if we hadn't been so busy with the recent crisis.'

Her words rang a bell. Guy had been going to talk to her about those two patients too, but subsequent events had stopped him. Now that the unit was getting back into some sort of routine, the problem attached to the pair of them had to be discussed.

Babs was still somewhat at a loss. From what she and Jane knew, and they worked with these patients more than anybody else, all was going well. Almost daily, there was minute but improved movement in Colin's leg, and Liz had positively blossomed on account of her friendship with Colin. They were virtually model patients. She said as much.

'Ah,' said Sister Crewe. 'That's what we professionals think, that they are both making excellent progress, due to the influence that each has over the other. I'm sorry to say, that our enthusiasm is not shared by their parents.'

'But why? Mr and Mrs Newbry were over the moon when Colin started to have some movement back in his leg. And, as for Mrs Pilbeam, she actually cried at the change in Liz, she was so thrilled.'

'Yes, I know that's true, but, you see, what they can't accept is that Colin and Liz have said that they love each other, and want to get married.'

'What?' Babs was astonished. Because of the pressure on the unit recently, all the normal duty rosters had been rather disrupted, but she was surprised that neither she nor Jane had been taken into their young patients' confidence. Not that that mattered. She was delighted for them. 'Gosh, they didn't waste any time, did they? I bet that's what their parents object to.'

'I think they agreed not to say anything while their parents thought it over and discussed the situation with doctors and counsellors,' explained Sister. 'That's the only reason that you haven't heard. You could be right, of course, in saying that's why their parents are so upset, though I think there's more to it than that.'

At that moment there was a tap at the door, and Guy entered.

He looked marvellous, cool, morning-fresh, in spite of the early heat, with his white shirt-sleeves rolled up above his elbows, and his uniform coat draped casually over his shoulders, ready to be shrugged on. His blue eyes seemed to speak volumes to Babs as he wished Sister and herself good morning.

Babs felt a constriction round her heart at the sight of him, but was able to return his greeting in a more or less formal voice.

'I was just filling Staff Nurse in on the situation relating to Colin Newbry and Liz Pilbeam,' said Sister.

Guy smiled at Babs in the most normal fashion, while she was still struggling to keep control over her bounding pulse at the pleasure of seeing him. She was acutely conscious of his nearness. It was infuriating that on the surface, at least, he seemed to be able to contain himself well, and the dancing, teasing expression in his eyes told her that he was well aware of how she felt. She bent her head and made a thing about examining some notes on the desk.

The phone rang, and Sister Crewe answered it.

Guy was still looking at her when she raised her head, his eyes full of suppressed humour, his mouth almost smiling. Determined to be as professional as he, she cleared her throat and said softly, so as not to interrupt Sister's telephone conversation, 'I don't understand what all this is about with Colin and Liz. You would think that their parents would be so pleased that they are happy that they wouldn't mind what happened.'

Guy grimaced. 'Convention, I'm afraid; that's what it's all about.'

'What do you mean — convention?'

'Well, none of the parents will come out with it directly, but I believe that Colin's mum and dad, and Liz's mum, can't take on board the fact that these two young people are sexually attracted to each other; they think it's rather indecent.'

'Because they are disabled or disfigured?'

'Exactly.'

'But that's monstrous. They're young, and otherwise healthy.'

'I know,' said Guy, smiling at Babs's defence of her

patients. 'But you see, we're used to seeing people who are physically imperfect, and sometimes emotionally disturbed, and know that underneath they are the same as anyone else. They're not. These accidents that have happened to their children are singular, dramatic, and I think that both the Newbrys and Mrs Pilbeam had resigned themselves to Colin and Liz being dependent upon them for the rest of their days. They can't readjust to the new situation.'

Sister finished with the telephone, and turned to Babs. 'Well, what do you think, Staff? How shall we tackle this problem, wait till the young people say something to us direct, or let them know that we understand how their parents feel?'

Babs had no doubts about it. 'We must wait until they're good and ready to talk to us; no way must we pressure them,' she said with certainty. 'For goodness' sake, they might even talk their parents round without anyone interfering. I know that that is what I should want to do if it were me and the man I loved.'

Guy gave her a wry smile, and Sister Crewe looked rather surprised at her passionate outburst.

Her vehemence made her go quite pink. She put a hand up to her hot cheek. 'I'm sorry, Sister,' she apologised. 'It's just that I feel so strongly about this. Because a person can't walk, or has something else wrong with them, able-bodied people assume that they can't think and have normal emotions, and we know that that's not true, don't we?' she appealed to her senior.

'We do, Staff, but you can't expect lay people to feel the same. The parents of this young couple are floundering. If their children don't need help, they do. We mustn't play God, but it is up to us to offer help and support all round. The families of our patients are as much our concern as our patients themselves. This is what rehabilitation is all about, don't you agree?'

It was Guy who answered. 'Yes, you're quite right, Sister, as always.' He gave the older woman a twinkling smile. 'We must offer help to the parents; that way we may best help Liz and Colin. But I also agree that we should give the couple concerned a chance to approach one of us themselves. I suggest that unless their folk put more pressure on us we should leave things for a day or two.' He added. 'A breathing space often helps.'

'I'll say amen to that,' said Sister Crewe. 'You have a wise head on young shoulders, Dr Lloyd.'

Guy inclined his head. He looked rather grave and not terribly young at that moment. 'Thank you, Sister, how kind,' he said. 'Now I'd best be getting on. I'd like to have a look at Basil Norton, please, our motor neurone patient.'

'Right, Doctor. Staff, will you go with Dr Lloyd, please, and then carry on with your work list once you have finished with Mr Norton.'

'Yes, Sister, will do.'

She and Guy walked down the corridor side by side. They stood aside to let someone go past with a trolley, and his hand brushed hers. She trembled very slightly.

'Have you managed,' she said in a rush, 'to think about tackling Jane?'

He said, not very enthusiastically, keeping her at a distance, 'Yes, I have, as a matter of fact, but I did tell you not to worry about it, so don't. As it happens, I'm seeing her tonight, and hope to have a rational discussion. Depending on the outcome, if I don't see you, I might give you a ring.' His coolness was rather daunting.

'I'll be at the club all evening, Guy. Roger and I are going to be practising like mad.'

'Sounds as if you're looking forward to it.' He gave her an unsmiling sideways look.

'You sound as if you're jealous,' she said in surprise.

'You'd better believe it,' he replied, in a half-teasing, half-serious manner. 'I can't tell you how much I envy him your company for the whole evening.'

Babs's heart raced with pleasure at his words.

They reached the day-room, where the cubicled beds were now occupied by previously warded patients. They stopped outside Basil Norton's cubicle.

Thrilled by his unexpected reply, she said, 'You don't really mind my playing with Roger, do you, Guy? After all, we've been partners all season, and I owe him tonight, on account of letting him down last night.'

'Is there any reason why I should mind?'

Surely he wasn't suspicious about her and Roger? It was ridiculous. If he was, it didn't show in his face. 'No, of course not,' she said quickly. 'It's just that I didn't explain properly about last night. I should have told him that I was going out for a meal with you, not been secretive about it, when there was no need.'

'Is that what's bothering you, that conscience of —?' He got no further; there was a thud and a muffled cry from behind the curtains, and then the sound of smothered swearing.

They swished back the curtain to reveal Basil lying on the floor between his bed and his chair. He was looking both embarrassed and furious.

'Hell,' he said. 'I was only trying to stand up, and my flaming ankle gave out.'

Guy and Babs leaned over him and Guy ran expert fingers down his legs and over his feet. 'Well, I don't think you've done any damage, old chap,' he said, smiling at the patient. 'But it'll teach you not to move without help or using some support. Bet you were trying to stand without even holding on to the locker, just to see if you could.'

'How the hell did you know that?'

'Believe it or not, we've come across blokes like you before, haven't we, Staff?'

'We certainly have,' said Babs, as she and Guy helped the man to his feet, and then sat him gently in the chair. 'You know,' she continued conversationally, 'it's great that you should try to help yourself, but do for heaven's sake do it sensibly. Hang on to things; that way you're likely to be independent longer, and you won't risk fracturing something in the process.'

Basil hung his head in mock-shame, his hazel eyes glinting with humour. 'Message received and understood. I hereby promise that I won't do anything so foolish again.' He smiled at them both. 'I don't know how you people do it,' he said, 'day after day looking after idiots like me.'

'Don't you know?' said Guy, smiling in return. 'It's for the marvellous salaries that we get paid, the short hours, and long, long holidays, isn't it, Staff?'

'Of course it is, Doctor. Why else would we put up with difficult patients like Mr Norton?'

It was just the sort of teasing that people like Basil responded to. It did him the world of good, relieving his tension, and enabling Guy to conduct his examination easily and judge more effectively the response of his muscles to various stimuli.

The examination took about twenty minutes, and Babs looked at her watch as she and Guy left the cubicle.

'Wow, I'll have to go like a bat out of hell to get through my list before lunch,' she said. 'And Jane and I have a full programme this afternoon. Guy, I must fly.'

'As any good bat would,' he said with a laugh. 'Babs, you are a delight.' He looked up and down the empty room, pulled her to himself very quickly, and kissed her on the tip of her nose. 'A taste of things to come,' he said, and then asked, almost sharply, 'You do love me, Babs, don't you? No half-measures?' His hands were still on her shoulders, his fingers biting hard into her soft flesh.

He was full of surprises today. She was excited by his fervency. She looked straight at him, her eyes full of tenderness. 'Guy, you know I do,' she said.

He looked thoughtful for a moment, then gave a brisk little nod, and his lips quirked at the corners in a half-smile as he said, low-voiced, 'Right, that's what I wanted to hear.'

Without another word, he turned on his heel and marched across the room and out of the door into the corridor.

Babs stood silently watching him go, her face soft with love. It had been a magic few moments, but if only he'd said that he loved her, instead of just hinting at it. It seemed that that was something else she would have to take on trust.

The rest of the day was hectic, and Jane, when Babs joined her in the hydrotherapy pool after lunch, was talkative. She rattled on about the previous evening, commenting several times on how funny it was that they had all ended up in the same place. But she seemed not the least bit suspicious, just bubbling over with good humour.

The last people in the pool that afternoon were Colin and Liz. Liz, with Colin's encouragement, had eventually consented to go into the pool, though she wore a thin cotton top to conceal her arm, over a conventional swimming-costume. This left just her badly scarred left leg exposed, but she appeared not to mind this, as long as there was no one else around except the four of them.

Just as they were about to leave the pool, Colin announced that there was something that he and Liz wanted to say to them.

'We think that you two ought to know,' he said, taking Liz's hand, 'that we're going to get married. You've both been such good mates; it seems only right that you should know.'

Babs feigned surprise, but Jane, who knew nothing of the way things had been going, was genuinely bowled over, and pleased as punch.

'I think it's absolutely super,' she said. 'And you're very wise not to hang about. Get married and make the most of it while you can; don't let any old fogies stop you. Don't you agree with that, Babs?'

Babs was genuinely surprised by Jane's enthusiasm, though it matched her own. 'I certainly do. Make up your own minds. You're both old enough. Do what you think is best for you,' she confirmed.

'It's great that you two feel like that. You see, our parents are dead against the idea.' Obviously they didn't know that their parents had confided in Guy and Sister Crewe.

'Then it's up to you to talk them round,' said Jane.

It was a pleasure to hear Jane give such strong support to their patients, but almost out of character. She was generally a cautious and rather conventional person, and it was surprising to see her so determined to back up Colin and Liz.

This was a different Jane from the woman who had once said that she would wait forever for Guy. What had brought this quick change of character about, and how would this Jane respond to what Guy was going to say to her tonight? Babs wondered.

She was jerked out of her puzzled thoughts by Jane herself.

'Can you spare a few minutes after work, Babs?' she asked as they made their way to the office to give their report to Sister. 'There's something that I want to tell you.'

What on earth can that be? thought Babs. I've had enough surprises for one day. She squashed a momentary panic lest it had to do with her and Guy, and said cheerfully, 'Of course. Let's get a cold drink and go and sit in the garden. I can do with some fresh air.'

'Me too, and I'm parched,' said Jane.

Some twenty minutes later they were seated in the little courtyard garden, enclosed on three sides by the rehab buildings. The grass was tinder-dry, and the sun blazed down. The air was hot and still, but they found a patch of shade beneath a tree, and they had the garden to themselves. Both girls sighed with pleasure as they kicked off their duty shoes and sat down on the grass.

Babs took a sip of her drink. 'Right, fire away,' she said, steeling herself for what she might hear.

Jane looked dreamily across the garden to where the herbaceous border blazed with vibrant red-hot pokers, brilliant orange montbretia and gaudy nasturtiums. They looked as if they thrived in the heat.

'Guy and I are going out tonight, Babs, and I think he wants to ask me to marry him. He was very insistent on it, even though it means we're missing a second evening's tennis practice. You and Roger are going to beat us hollow in the finals if we reach them, I'm afraid.' She didn't sound as if she minded very much.

Babs felt her heart sink. This was terrible, it was the worst possible scenario for what Guy was going to say to Jane if she thought that he was going to propose.

Quaking inwardly, but making her voice steady, she asked, 'What makes you think he's going to do that? You know what men are, making such odd things sound important. He probably wants to ask you to go to a cricket match with him, or something equally trivial.'

She tried to think of something else to say — anything. She opened her mouth to speak, when Jane, who was still looking over the garden, lost in her own private dream, said, quite cheerfully, 'The trouble is, Babs, I don't want to marry Guy, not any more.'

Babs choked on her drink.

'What do you mean?' she asked stupidly, as if the words hadn't been plain enough. She tried to put some sense into her remark by adding, 'Have you met someone else?' A wave of hope washed over her; what a marvellous solution to all their problems, if this were the answer.

'No,' said Jane, and laughed. 'Nothing like that, more's the pity. I wish I could find someone, like you've found Roger. You make such a super pair.'

Babs swallowed her astonishment. 'But Roger and I are just good friends,' she said weakly.

'That's what they all say,' said Jane with a grin. 'But you can't fool me. He might be like an iceberg with everyone else, but he's different with you.'

Babs said firmly, 'I promise you that Roger and I haven't anything going between us. But you and Guy have been in love for yonks — since you were kids, you said.'

'We thought we were,' said Jane decisively. 'But I realise now that it was just kids' stuff, and we've been pretending since we grew up.'

'I see,' she said weakly, not seeing at all and feeling completely lost.

Jane was babbling on about going to Australia with her friend Trish, and how on earth she was going to break the news to Guy, when, white coat flapping, he suddenly appeared in the sun-baked garden.

All three of them were surprised.

Guy recovered first. 'Oh, so this is where rehab staff skive off to when they want a break, is it?' he said in a commendably teasing fashion.

'We're off duty,' said Babs and Jane in unison, recovering their composure.

'Oh, really?' Guy laughed. 'Tell that to the marines.'

Both girls laughed and shied their empty cartons at him. He bent to retrieve them, muttering, 'Litter louts,' under his breath, but Babs guessed that he was playing for time and hiding his surprise at meeting up with them so unexpectedly.

'Actually,' he said, as he straightened up, 'I'm glad that I've caught you, Jane. Do you mind if we meet up a bit later this evening than we planned? The casualty registrar has asked me to stand in for him till about eight, but that probably means nearer nine.'

Jane said happily, 'Oh, I don't mind. Look, Guy, why don't we put our dinner off to another evening? We should get in some tennis practice anyway, and even if you can't get there before it's too dark I could.'

If Guy was surprised by Jane's suggestion, he covered it well.

'Good idea,' he said easily. 'We'll fix something for later in the week.' He bent down and brushed her cheek with his lips. 'Bye, love,' he said. 'Thanks for understanding about tonight.'

'One gets used to it with you doctors,' replied Jane with a theatrical sigh.

As soon as Guy had disappeared into the building she turned to Babs, her face and eyes shining with happiness.

'Do you know,' she said, 'I don't think that it's going

to be so bad telling Guy how I feel. I think perhaps he knows already and is prepared for it.'

'What makes you think that?'

'Sixth sense, or something,' said Jane. She looked thoughtful. 'I know him so well.'

Babs recalled that Guy had talked about Jane's sixth sense. She said, trying to be practical and to squash her feeling of elation that the Jane business might be resolved once and for all, 'Why don't you fix yourself up with another tennis partner and join Roger and me at the club this evening? We plan to have a really hard work-out, and it would be great if you were there, even if Guy can't be.'

'Love to,' said Jane, as if she hadn't a care in the world. 'You know, Babs, it's such a relief to have fallen out of love with Guy. I feel free for the first time in years.' She stood up. 'I'll just whiz off home and get my things, and see you in about an hour's time.'

'Great,' said Babs, feeling shattered by Jane's confession. 'See you then.'

They parted, Jane going to the car park, and Babs making for the nurses' home, deep in thought, pondering the extraordinary events of the last half-hour, and how they would affect herself and Guy.

CHAPTER TEN

BABS walked slowly back through the hot, dusty gardens, feeling lethargic and sluggish now that the first euphoria of the news that Jane had given her was beginning to wear off. Her mood matched the weather, which was heavily oppressive. The deep blue sky was faintly tinged with bronze, as if a storm was brewing, and the air was uncomfortably humid. Just as the gardens need rain, she thought wryly, so I need a shower. For once she was not looking forward to playing tennis.

She had seldom felt so unsure of herself. Should she let Guy know about Jane's change of heart so that he was forewarned before he spoke to her? No, she realised immediately, she couldn't do that, for, though Jane hadn't said that she was speaking to her in confidence, it had been implied. She would just have to let matters take their course. They were out of her hands and firmly into Guy's, capable as they were, where, in fact, he had insisted that the problem should be.

This was some small comfort, but she remained cross with herself for feeling deflated. It didn't seem right. She should have been feeling great, but for some reason she wasn't. She was apprehensive, bothered by tiny pinpricks of doubt about herself and Guy, and a future together. She gave herself a mental shake, and resolved not to think such rubbish, reminding herself how certain Guy had been that all would be well.

The thought cheered and reassured her somewhat, and she felt rather better after she'd taken a long, cooling shower, washed her hair, and changed into her tennis gear. But she couldn't quite shake off the feeling of unease, however hard she tried, though she told herself repeatedly, as she made her way slowly to the clubhouse, that there was no cause for her misgivings. What made it worse, of course, was that there was no concrete reason why she should not at this moment be feeling ecstatically happy, and why she wasn't was a mystery that she couldn't define. Try as she might, she couldn't dismiss her muddled, unhappy thoughts.

Because she had dawdled, and had taken her time with her shower, she was a little late meeting Roger, and full of apologies.

'It doesn't matter, Babs,' he said. 'You're here now. Look, I've bagged a court; let's get out there and play.'

They walked in silence towards the tennis courts, baking dustily in the early evening sunshine. The dry grass shimmered with the day's stored heat. Babs's mind continued to turn over and over her uncomfortable thoughts relating to herself and Guy, as she tried to make sense out of them.

Roger gave her a sideways glance, which she missed.

'By the way,' said Babs suddenly, breaking the silence as they let themselves into a court, 'Jane's joining us presently. Guy's working, and she's going to find another partner to practise with until he can get here.'

'Oh, splendid,' said Roger in his usual drawl. 'Let's

hope that it's someone who can at least hit a ball.' Then, in a most unlikely gesture for him, he put a hand on Babs's shoulder. 'Are you all right, my dear?' he asked, this time without the drawl. 'You seem rather *distraite*.'

Roger was such a remote sort of man that his words and the fact that he had touched her made Babs realise what a bad job she was making of concealing her feelings. She made a great effort to pull herself together; after all, she owed Roger her full attention tonight after letting him down last evening. She produced one of her dimpling smiles. 'I'm fine, thanks, just a bit headachey; must be the weather.' She fanned herself with her hands, trying to stir the hot, breathless air into some kind of movement. 'But I'll feel better once we start playing.'

'Good girl, that's more like it. I'd like to get really stuck in this evening and beat the hell out of whoever we play; what about you?'

'Yes, I feel the same; let's get cracking.'

He lifted her spirits with his determination to win and his uncomplaining attitude over her being late. Roger, she guessed, would always go out to be a winner, and he didn't suffer fools gladly, but he wasn't quite as stiff and unapproachable as some people imagined. She determined to make up for last night's lost practice match by playing brilliantly tonight.

Jane turned up a few minutes after they started knocking up, with a new young houseman, Tom Butcher. He played well, though not up to Guy's standard, but his efforts, combined with Jane's uninhibited, carefree play, which seemed to Babs to indicate her friend's new-found confidence, resulted in a good match.

Guy arrived just after half-past eight, as Tom was going back on duty. Babs's heart missed a beat as she saw him enter the court, and all her earlier misgivings drained away at the sight of him, so tall and fair and handsome. He looked totally confident, as if he could cope with anything, even her silly apprehensions. His brief white shorts showed off his tanned muscled legs to perfection, and the thin cotton shirt moulded to his torso emphasised the breadth of his chest and shoulders. He was a man to be reckoned with, who could handle anything, and who could certainly manage the forthcoming meeting with Jane.

Babs heaved a great sigh of relief. She had nothing to worry about.

'Evening,' he called as he took the cover off his racket, looking up at the darkening sky. 'Might get in a few rallies before light fails. Sorry I couldn't make it before.'

'It's OK,' said Roger. 'We've had quite a decent match. Young Butcher's not half bad, and Jane played like a demon.'

'Yes, I can believe that,' replied Guy, and he and Jane exchanged what Babs thought was a meaningful look.

Perhaps, she thought, Jane's right, and Guy has got some idea about her change of heart. It seemed incredible, but not impossible, considering how well they knew each other. Probably even last night in the Portsmouth pub Guy had been beginning to pick up pointers as to Jane's feelings. No wonder he's so confident about making his own position clear, she thought.

'Babs, snap out of it,' called Guy across the net. 'We're ready to begin.'

Babs quelled her rampant thoughts. 'Oh, sorry,' she apologised to her partner and their opponents. 'I'm with you now. Let's go; your service.'

She made up for her lack of concentration before the match by playing superbly well during the few games they were able to complete before bad light stopped play altogether. She smashed and sliced and volleyed the ball with amazing energy and accuracy. Whether it was Guy's presence, or suddenly getting the right perspective on today's events, she didn't know. She was only aware of a great swell of confidence engulfing her and smothering any reservations that she had had about the future. It was a wonderful feeling, and she and Roger won the short match, largely by her efforts, by five games to two.

For the second time that evening Roger put an arm round her and squeezed her shoulder.

'Well done, partner,' he drawled. 'Play like that in the finals and we'll beat these two hollow.'

'Like hell you will,' said Guy. 'But the lady is to be congratulated on her fabulous play.' He bent and kissed her cheek in what seemed to be a casual manner, but his blue eyes met hers briefly, and seemed to speak volumes that his friendly kiss hadn't conveyed. She put a foot up on the bench and made a thing out of fastening her shoelace while she regained her calm, and, with a small smile playing round his mouth, Guy moved away to speak to Roger.

Jane strolled over and stood beside her.

'Yes, congratulations, Babs, super play,' she said, and, as Babs straightened up, added softly, 'As Guy and I had to scrub tonight's confidential chat, I thought I'd suggest that we have a practice game early tomorrow, and then I'll put him in the picture about everything. It will be easier here than in a restaurant over a meal, and anyway, I don't want to wait for a free evening. What do you think?'

'Great idea; good luck.'

'Thanks.'

A few minutes later the four of them started to walk back to the clubhouse, discussing the game ball by ball.

Jane took Guy's arm, and said with a laugh, 'If we don't want to get clobbered again by this super pair here, I think we'd better get in some extra practice before the draw for the competition matches tomorrow night, don't you?'

'Good idea,' he said briskly. 'Seven o'clock tomorrow morning; give me an hour before I start my rounds.'

'Great, suits me,' said Jane, giving Babs a small conspiratorial smile.

Babs thought that Guy had agreed almost too readily to the arrangement, and wondered if he was aware that Jane planned more than a game of tennis. Not that it mattered if he did; the important thing was that he should hear her story, and tell his own.

It was hot and oppressive. A light, unpleasant wind was blowing in small gusts, powdering everything with a fine white dust from the chalkpits on the downs. The sky was darkening from purple to indigo.

'Going to have a storm by the look of it,' said Roger, pointing to a line of woolly dark clouds massing over the nearby hills. 'That'll be a relief all round.'

They all four stopped to look at the ominous clouds building up on the skyline close by, beginning to move rapidly before the wind.

'It's going to absolutely pelt down in a few minutes,' said Guy. 'Jane, I don't think we should stop off at the clubhouse. You know you don't like thunderstorms; I'd better get you back to the village.'

Was it a ruse to get Jane alone, and talk tonight? Babs wondered.

There was a rumble of distant thunder, and a sheet of lightning illuminated the tops of the hills.

Jane went quite white. 'Yes, please,' she said to Guy. She turned to Babs and Roger. 'I hate thunderstorms,' she said between gritted teeth. 'They tend to give me a migraine. Do you mind if we give the drinks a miss?'

'Of course not; you get off at once,' said Roger. 'Do you want anything to help you to sleep? I'm sure Guy or I could write you up for something.'

'No, thanks. I'll be fine once I'm inside the house.' She gave a shaky laugh. 'I can always put my head under the pillow and say my prayers.'

'You do that,' said Roger. 'It's probably as good a cure as anything that we can offer. You'd better both get moving before the rain arrives. Goodnight, see you on court in the finals.'

They all laughed and exchanged goodnights. Guy was holding Jane's hand, but Babs knew that it was only a friendly and comforting gesture, and the look in his eyes when they fleetingly met hers confirmed this. He loves me, she thought on a rising tide of fresh happiness; he really loves me, even if he hasn't actually said so. She regretted that she had to stand, paired with Roger, exchanging pleasantries.

Jane and Roger were talking as she stared mesmerised into Guy's blue, blue eyes. Voices faded into a murmur, making no sense. There was a buzzing in her ears, blotting out all sound. Guy put out a hand and touched hers briefly, lightly. Her lips mouthed his name. Guy. . . She felt breathless.

Roger took hold of her arm, and said something. She tore her eyes away from Guy's and blinked. She glanced at Roger and Jane. Had they noticed the long look that had passed between herself and Guy? No, of course not. She smiled at Jane and repeated her goodnights, and a few minutes later they parted, Jane and Guy to go to the car park, she and Roger to the clubhouse.

She felt numbed by her silent exchange with Guy, but her mind wouldn't stop churning. He must love her as she loved him. In a few hours he would be free to love her openly. Yet once again, in spite of what his eyes had told her, there was still that strange and nagging suggestion in the back of her mind that she shouldn't give in at once. That she shouldn't commit herself. Why? she asked silently. Why? She could find no answer.

They were nearly at the clubhouse. Roger must think it strange that she was so silent. It was incredible that he hadn't noticed anything between her and Guy. She must think of something normal to say.

'Poor Jane,' she blurted out. 'It must be horrid to be so affected by a storm. Funnily enough, I rather enjoy them.'

Roger replied. 'Yes, quite a lot of people are badly affected, especially if they are migraine sufferers.' He took her arm. 'Look,' he said, 'if we don't hurry we're going to get soaked.'

Even as he spoke, large drops of rain plopped down on them.

'Come on,' he said, tugging her along. He broke into a run, and she jogged beside him till they reached the clubhouse.

Babs shivered as they sat down in the cane chairs at a table for two.

'My goodness,' she said, 'the temperature has dropped suddenly.' She pulled the cardigan that she had brought with her out of her bag, and draped it round her shoulders. 'Gosh, that's better.'

'I recommend a warming drink for once,' said Roger. 'A whisky. What about it, Babs?'

'I'll take a wee dram with you, Mr Mansfield,' replied Babs in a teasing Scottish accent, determined not to let her seething thoughts spoil the rest of the evening. She owed at least that to Roger.

'There's nae so good as a wee dram,' retaliated Roger, a soft Highland lilt in his voice, 'to warm the cockles, or anything else for that matter.'

He went away to fetch the drinks. There was quite a crush at the bar, and Babs's thoughts returned to the problem of Jane and Guy and herself while she waited for his return. The eternal triangle, she thought. Yet I shouldn't feel like that. It isn't really a triangle any more; Jane's change of heart has altered all that. It's just my feelings now that are a problem. How can you love someone the way I love Guy, yet be afraid to commit yourself? The question hung in the air, in her mind.

She became aware of Roger standing looking down at her, glasses in his hand.

'They look as if they're worth more than a penny,' he said in his rather dry manner.

Babs looked puzzled. 'I'm sorry,' she said. 'I don't understand.'

Roger put a drink in front of her and sat down in the chair opposite. He leaned across and tapped her forehead gently. 'Your thoughts,' he repeated, 'are worth more than a penny.'

'They are to me,' said Babs with a laugh. 'But I'm sorry; you must think me awfully rude, sitting here daydreaming.'

'No, but you look sad, and that's not like you. You've been rather pensive for much of the evening, though you managed to play well enough to beat the opposition. Babs, can I help? Do you want to talk about it?'

'Oh.' The suggestion, coming from him, startled her. Only a few hours before she had wished that there was someone around in whom she might confide; now he seemed to be here in the unlikely shape of Roger Mansfield, offering a listening ear. Clever Roger Mansfield, who seemed to know the answer to so many things, a man with few friends, full of dry-as-dust facts; but was he a suitable person to help her with her emotional problems regarding Guy? And did she, in fact, now want him to help her?

He was a doctor, used to keeping confidences; he knew both herself and Guy as well as his ivory tower existence allowed. He might not be an ideal person to dish out advice, but at least he would be an ideal person to confide in.

'Well?' Roger was sipping his drink and watching her closely. 'Do you want to come clean, dear girl, and tell Uncle all about it?' He gave her the rare lop-sided grin which made such a difference to his normally rather severe and uninviting expression.

'All right,' said Babs, suddenly making up her mind. 'I will. But I hope that I don't bore you to death.'

'Never,' said Roger firmly. 'Nothing you have to say would ever bore me; don't you know that?'

Babs didn't even try to answer that surprising double-edged remark. She couldn't believe that he was evenly obliquely suggesting that he cared for her in any but the most casual manner.

She plunged straight into her story. 'Well, first of all, I have a confession to make about last night.'

'A confession? That sounds dramatic.'

'Yes, well, maybe that's an exaggeration. I just wanted to tell you that I went out for a meal with Guy last night; that's why I cancelled our game. I'm sorry; it was rather mean of me to do that at the last minute and not be honest about it.'

'Perhaps you only got the invite at the last minute, Babs, and in any case you don't owe me an explanation. We're good friends, and friends should be able to say yea or nay to each other when necessary.'

'Thank you. I'm glad you understand.'

Roger slipped into a Socttish accent again. 'Now what else, lassie, is it that you want to have a good old blether about?'

Hearing him say 'blether', just like her Scottish granny did, made it suddenly easier.

'It's about Guy and me,' she said. 'We're in love with each other; we have been ever since we first met, though we didn't realise it then. Well, I didn't anyway, and Guy wouldn't say anything because there was a problem, but now that doesn't exist any more there's no reason why we shouldn't. . .'

Words failed her. How on earth could she explain to this austere man that she had reservations about forming a physical relationship with Guy? He would probably assume, in his clinical fashion, that she had some sexual hang-up, and nothing could be further from the truth, especially where Guy was concerned. Could she make Roger understand that it was because she wanted Guy so badly in every sort of way that she didn't want to trivialise it by having a casual affair? And yet that, in spite of wanting him so badly, she didn't feel ready to commit herself to him forever? He would probably dismiss her muddled thoughts as the emotional meanderings of a silly young woman.

The trouble was, she wasn't used to talking about herself and her feelings, though she'd often advised patients to do just that. She had been brought up to keep her own counsel, find her own solutions to her problems, not wear her heart on her sleeve and expect other people to come to her aid.

Roger reached across the table and took hold of her

hands. It seemed to be a night for him to touch her. 'Babs, you don't have to tell me if you don't want to. I offered to listen, to help, not make things more difficult. We'll say no more about it if that's what you wish. Now come on, swallow that down and have another dram.' He put the glass to her lips and she gulped down the remainder of the whisky, and, in spite of the heat of the room, and the thunder crashing around the building, she was grateful for the glow that stole through her, warming her cold insides.

Roger went away to get fresh drinks, and within a few moments was back with another whisky for her and a lager for himself.

'Yours is medicinal; you need it,' he said as he took in her surprised look.

Babs took a tiny sip from her glass, and made up her mind for the second time to talk.

'Roger, I do want your advice, or at least your willingness to listen. I feel I've reached a crossroads in my life, an important crossroads, and the decision I make will affect not only me and my career, but Guy, and perhaps his career too.' She looked down at her glass, and then back at Roger, facing him squarely. 'You see, I don't want to hurt him; I love him too much. I don't want to refuse him anything, but I'm simply not sure if I can commit myself at this point.'

'And is Guy demanding commitment?'

'That's the trouble; I don't really know. We haven't had time to talk much about how we feel, because——'

'Until now there's been a more tangible problem to be overcome?'

'Yes, that's it exactly.'

'And now you've got to face up to your own reservations about a relationship, which you were able to ignore before.'

'Yes.'

'Babs,' he said, in a flat, almost bored voice, 'you don't need to talk to me, or anybody else, except Guy. Tell him exactly how you feel; don't hold anything back. If he loves you as much as you love him, you'll find a solution, but only if you're honest with each other.'

'Oh, Roger, you are a sweetie.' She stopped and blushed, and thought how ridiculous it was to use such a phrase to describe Roger. He was sarcastic, and abrasive, and totally without Guy's charisma or charm, but he was being helpful. She said in a softer tone, 'Thanks for listening; thanks for the advice. You're absolutely right, of course. I must be honest; I was just too muddled to see it. Honesty is always the best policy, as my old granny would undoubtedly say. You know, in a strange sort of way, you remind me of her.' She giggled. It was as much with relief as anything. 'I don't mean in looks, of course, but in your. . .'

'Elderly wisdom,' said Roger drily.

'Yes, I suppose that that is what I mean.' She was deadly serious again. 'Roger, I am most grateful. It was there, staring me in the face, yet I couldn't see it. Isn't it funny? One hears patients saying that sort of thing so often after they've had counselling or just talked freely to anyone, and yet I couldn't see how it applied to Guy and me, till you pointed it out.'

'What are friends for,' said Roger, his usual drawling, sarcastic voice almost gentle, 'if not to be around when needed?' He leaned across the table, and, incredibly, brushed his lips across her forehead. 'Guy,' he said softly, 'is a very lucky guy.'

CHAPTER ELEVEN

BABS slept soundly all night, and woke to brilliant sunshine and skies of rain-washed periwinkle-blue.

She let memories of last night ripple over her as she struggled into wakefulness. She had gone to bed with her racing thoughts, not expecting to sleep after the emotional events of the day, and in fact had dropped off immediately with the thunderstorm crashing round her.

'Must have been the whisky,' she mumbled wryly a few minutes later as she stood under the shower.

The first needles of tepid water woke her thoroughly, and, with the sharpening of her senses, she was reminded with a jolt that today was going to be special, following the meeting between Guy and Jane. Her tummy churned at the prospect. It was both wonderful and frightening at the same time. The thought of being free to love Guy was exhilarating; the thought of what Guy might expect, and her own uncertainty as to how she might react, still niggled away.

She hung on to what Roger had said last night about talking everything through with Guy, and knew that it was the right thing to do.

It was seven o'clock, and Guy and Jane would be on the tennnis court by now, ostensibly for their practice match, but in reality for Jane's big confession.

She decided to go to the refectory for breakfast

instead of having a scratch meal of toast and coffee in the house kitchen. Nerves made her feel hungry, and there was the added attraction of going there on the off chance that Guy might call in after his game, and be able to pass on his news. He would surely make an effort to see her as soon as possible. She hated the thought that she might have to go on duty without knowing the outcome of the morning's meeting, although there was really no reason to suspect that it wouldn't go off smoothly, since Jane and Guy wanted the same thing: their freedom.

She had nearly finished eating, sitting at a secluded corner table for two, when she was surprised to see not Guy, but Jane appear. Jane saw Babs, and made directly for her.

'Babs, may I join you?' It was a polite nothing, for she sat down before Babs could answer. 'I hoped that I might find you here; I thought that you'd like to know what happened between Guy and me. We both planned to come over for breakfast, but he was bleeped, and has had to go hungry to work, poor man.' She pulled a comic face, and then smiled happily.

This was the ebullient, sparkling Jane speaking, who had so surprised Babs yesterday. This Jane seemed to have shed some heavy load, which in a way was true, as she was no longer burdened with love for a man who couldn't return it, thought Babs.

'Did you manage to have your heart-to-heart before Guy was called away?'

'Oh, rather. And you know how afraid I was of hurting him because I'd realised that I was no longer in love with him?'

Babs nodded.

'Well, it seems that he'd begun to feel the same, you know. He even hinted that he'd found someone else.'

Babs choked on her coffee.

'So it wasn't such a traumatic meeting after all?' she asked after clearing her throat. 'You did say that he might have guessed part at least of what you had to say.'

'It was marvellous. It was all over in a few minutes. I said my piece and Guy said his, and we laughed a lot, and I cried a bit, because it was the end of a childhood dream, and that was that really. And Guy approves wholeheartedly of my going off to Australia to work; well, that's if they'll have me. But I shall go over anyway with Trish for a holiday to get the feel of the place.'

'But isn't she going in about six weeks' time?'

'Yes, but I have nearly three weeks' leave due, and I'm going to give in my month's notice today, so with luck I'll only have a week or so to work. And I know that I can get a seat on Trish's flight, because her boyfriend was going with her to see her settled, but has to back out because of his work. I shall take up his passage.'

Her decisiveness, her enthusiasm, shook Babs.

'I'm going to miss you at work, and as a friend,' she said sincerely. 'It's a hell of a big step to take, Jane; are you sure about it?'

'Quite sure. Oh, don't think that I'm going without qualms,' said Jane. 'I shall miss you and the work, and, of course, Guy, but perhaps what I've learned here at

Princes Park will serve me well, and I'll have something new to offer down under.'

Babs said, 'Oh, I'm sure you will, and I wish you the very best of luck; it's a tremendous thing to do.' She looked at her watch, and groaned. 'I must dash or I'll be late for report.'

It was an excuse to bring the conversation to an end. In fact she had a few minutes to spare, so she dawdled in the already hot sunshine as she walked from the refectory to the unit. In spite of the heat, last night's storm had cleared the air and freshened the grass and plants, washing the white chalk dust away. Everything smelt good and seemed to be crackling with new life. Fancifully, she wondered if it might be a good omen.

She guessed that Guy had hinted at being in love with someone to make Jane feel happier about turning him down. He was making sure that she didn't have to feel anything like pity for him — something that he, with his strong, masculine pride, would have found insupportable. Well, Babs mused, it suited her not to have Guy making known her love for him, even in confidence to Jane. Until she had had the frank conversation with him that Roger had suggested, the fewer people who knew of her feelings, the better.

If things changed before Jane left, she would tell her herself that she and Guy had been in love for some time. Meanwhile she was happy to let matters drift.

The morning, like most mornings in Rehab, passed quickly and busily, and even Guy's arrival just after nine o'clock went by almost unnoticed by Babs. They only had time to acknowledge each other with a wave across the patient-filled hydrotherapy pool, as he was on his way to the children's pool.

The small children had their own pool, where they played with — and unconsciously helped treat themselves by using — the water toys provided. Some sat astride fat, blown-up imitations of porpoises and turtles to help them spread their hips in otherwise painful exercises, hips that were for the most part congenitally deformed and wouldn't respond to other treatment, but which had to be forced apart if any sort of improvement could be made. Relaxing in the warm, buoyant water with funny animals to use made this more possible, less painful, and could even be fun.

There were many aides about, as well as physiotherapists and nurses, as great care was taken to ensure the children's safety as they worked and played.

In the adult pool it was 'briny day'; that was the day when properly measured quantities of saline were added to the pool, to help and stimulate the rheumatic patients who benefited from this treatment.

Here too, plenty of staff were around to assist patients in the pool. It was very satisfying to see people of all ages, who walked stiffly and painfully on terra firma, moving easily in the water. Most of them loved it, and enjoyed the gentle massage that followed. For patients from the day clinic it was also a social occasion, since many of them lived alone and weren't very mobile. Visiting Princes for the day, having a warm swim, chatting to other patients and the cheerful staff, and then enjoying a good lunch, was an outing not to be missed.

It was one of the clinics that Babs most enjoyed,

because here even hopelessly chronic patients could enjoy a little respite from their condition.

As it happened, Jane had been seconded to the outpatients clinic for the morning, after she'd had her interview with the administrator and handed in her notice, so Babs hadn't seen her since their conversation at breakfast. Neither, to her disappointment, did she see anything more of Guy after her fleeting glimpse of him as he passed through the department. He got called away just as he finished assessing the children, and didn't visit the adult pool at all.

Although she was busy answering questions and encouraging patients to move rigid limbs, one part of her mind refused to stop working on a personal level. She mulled over Jane's report of her conversation with Guy. What a blessing that everything had turned out so well for them both, with no hang-ups or recriminations, after years of being close to each other.

If only Guy and I can sort ourselves out as happily, life will be marvellous, she thought, and the sooner we can talk to each other and do this, the better.

The busy morning eventually came to an end, and Sister sent her to lunch. She hurried down the long main corridor, hoping that she might meet up with Guy in the refectory. A few moments later she saw him striding towards her, coat flapping, stethoscope hanging half out of a pocket.

He came to a halt as they drew level.

'Hello, Babs,' he said with a smile that, as always, made her heart beat faster. 'I'm glad I met up with you; we must talk.'

'Yes,' she said, trying to sound as confident as he. 'We must.'

If only she could be sure that he was as affected by her as she was by him. Was his heart hammering in his chest just because she was close? Were his hands clammy and trembling? She looked at his hands and his face, but neither gave anything away. Why couldn't he, just for once, reveal his true feelings? And why wasn't she sure that hers were strong enough to override her career ambitions? What if he demanded more than she could give? Her muddled thoughts gathered momentum. How ridiculous it was that, now that the Jane business was over, her own uncertainties were producing another obstacle to her relationship with Guy.

He took hold of her arm, and she felt the fine hairs on it rise as he touched her. She looked sideways at him, but his face was impassive. 'Let's go outside,' he said, drawing her through the open French windows, into the rose garden. 'I want to talk about Colin and Liz; they're in a dreadful state.'

His words shook her rigid. He wanted to talk about patients, when she had thought that he meant a personal conversation! For a moment, words failed her; then she did what she had so often had to do in her professional life — swallow her disappointment and concentrate on her patients.

'Why? I thought things were beginning to improve for them. What's wrong now?'

'Well, as you know, the parents on both sides are dead against this marriage, but we all thought that, given time, they could be won over. Apparently we

were wrong, and it seems that they mean business.
Liz's mum wants to take her home, and the point is,
she is practically ready to be discharged till its time to
start more plastic surgery. There's no reason why she
shouldn't go home and wait there for further treatment.
Mrs Pilbeam's no fool; she knows this.'

'But can't they see how cruel this would be, to split
up these two who have helped each other so much?'

'They may see it, but don't want to know it. They
think they know what's best for them. I think they feel
that if they separate them their love for each other will
just fade away.'

'That's not fair; they wouldn't think that if they were
both quite fit and healthy.'

'Probably not, but convention is a hard taskmaster.
They're probably wondering what the neighbours will
say if someone who is disfigured marries someone who
is half paralysed. People with those sorts of disabilities
are not supposed to have ordinary feelings.'

They sat down on one of the garden seats, shaded by
a weeping laburnum tree, but clearly visible from the
corridor and other parts of the building.

Guy said, allowing himself to be personal for a
moment, his voice heavy with irony, and one eyebrow
raised as he looked towards the many windows over
looking the garden, 'Well, no one can accuse us of
having a secret lovers' meeting.'

'Perhaps we would be wise to keep it this way until
we're both sure how things are going to work out,' said
Babs, in a small, uncertain voice.

Guy didn't show any surprise at her comment, but
said firmly, 'We haven't had a chance yet to discuss our

personal affairs, and this is not the time or the place. Let's meet this evening and get everything sorted.' He looked closely at Babs. 'You have heard, presumably, from Jane what happened this morning?'

Their eyes caught and held. 'Yes,' whispered Babs. 'She told me.'

'Ah, I thought that she might have done.' His eyes held hers for a moment longer, and Babs was sure that he knew that she had known about Jane's change of heart before their meeting. He stretched his long legs out in front of him, and folded his arms across his chest. 'Now,' he said, 'enough of us for the moment; we've got to think of Colin and Liz.'

'Yes, what are we going to do to help them?' she said briskly.

'Get help from social services, see if they might fix up somewhere for them to live, where they can have help,' replied Guy. 'And get the chaplain to visit them and arrange to marry them. That's what they want.'

Babs's resolve to be entirely professional deserted her. She looked down at her hands linked in her lap. 'It must be marvellous,' she said softly, 'to be so sure.'

Guy gave her a sharp look. 'Why aren't you sure, Babs?' he said. 'Now that this business with Jane is out of the way.'

'I don't know,' said Babs, and to her horror her voice wobbled. 'It's just that. . .' She took out her small handkerchief and blew her nose.

'You're afraid that it won't work out for us?' He was watching her in a detached manner, and appeared unmoved by the fact that she was near to tears.

'No — yes. It's just that I don't know whether I can

commit myself, and if I can't I'd rather not start anything. Anyway, it's not all me. I. . . I just don't know how you feel; you seem to be too calm about everything, too clinical, too calculating.'

She couldn't keep down the rising tide of anger now that she had started to let go. All the frustrations of the past weeks came to a head. She remembered his passion that day in Sister's office, but she remembered too the earlier time by the pool, when he had rejected her. She recalled how calmly he had taken the disappointment of finding Jane in the Portsmouth pub, which for her had ruined the evening, but which had seemed to have little effect on him. His reactions hadn't been those of a man wildly in love, so perhaps what he felt for her was just a physical, sexual thing.

He said, in a quiet, even voice, 'I repeat what I said before, Babs; this is neither the time nor the place for a personal discussion. Perhaps we do both have reservations, but whatever we have to say to each other cannot be said here, or in a hurry. Let's postpone it till we can meet properly; we owe that much to ourselves.' His eyes were full of compassion, belying the unemotional tone in his voice. Perhaps he did care—a little, anyway. He drew a large white handkerchief from his trouser pocket and handed it to her. 'Here,' he said, and this time his voice was full of tolerant humour. 'Yours is all used up. Have another good blow; it'll make you feel better. Then we'll get back to the matter in hand—Colin and Liz—and see if we can thrash out a plan of action.'

Suddenly Babs felt better. Guy as the good doctor and friend was easy to understand, and what he said made sense. She blew her nose hard and gave him a watery smile as she tucked his handkerchief away into her uniform pocket.

'I'll launder it, and let you have it back nicely ironed,' she said.

Guy grinned broadly. 'Well, praise be,' he said with a chuckle. 'I just hate ironing.'

Babs reached out and touched his hand. 'Thanks,' she said softly. 'I'm sure that we're going to work things out.' She straighted her shoulders; she felt suddenly optimistic. 'Now, about Colin and Liz. We thought that time and a breathing space would help their parents come round, but it doesn't seem to have worked. I think you're right, Guy; we've got to do something constructive, like getting the chaplain in on this, and helping them get married before their parents break them up.'

'Right,' said Guy, at his briskest and most professional. 'I'll have a word with Sister and the chaplain, and we'll set the ball rolling. Time and patience with the parents haven't got us anywhere; let's see what a little positive action will do.' He looked at his watch. 'Lord, I must be on my way.' He stood up and stretched and then bent down to speak softly in her ear. 'Babs, don't let our personal affairs get you down. I'll sort things out, never fear.' He raised a hand in a farewell salute, and walked back through the garden, where the scented, overblown roses nodded in the afternoon heat.

Babs watched him go with mixed feelings. She wanted to believe what he had said about everything getting sorted out. She half believed that he would do it. He was good at sorting out other people's problems;

half his work was concerned with that. It wasn't just getting patients to their best physical peak, no matter what their condition, but building up their morale to match. That was something that he was supremely good at.

She was sure that in the end he would be successful where Colin and Liz were concerned. She was not so sure that he could achieve a happy end result on the personal front. Like other people, he and she needed time too. Perhaps that was the trouble: they were pushing things too fast. After all, they had only known each other a little over two months. Ten weeks and two days, actually, said a voice in her head; ten weeks and two days exactly.

She got up from the garden seat. There was still time to snatch a sandwich, only she didn't feel in the least bit hungry. I might as well go back on duty, she decided, and made her way to the rehab unit.

CHAPTER TWELVE

THE afternoon was as busy as the morning, and Babs found herself on ward duties, which entailed caring for those patients at present on afternoon bed rest with treatment.

She had just finished dressing the suppurating ulcer of a diabetic patient on reassessment of diet and medication when Sister Crewe sent a senior student for her with instructions that the student should carry on with her list, while Babs went to the office.

'I was just going to start on Tommy, the cystic fibrosis boy,' Babs explained. 'Do you know how to do his pummelling treatment?'

'Yes, Staff, I've done it twice before under the physio's instruction.'

'Fine, you know what you're about, then. Carry on there, and if I'm not back take Mrs King—that's the dear old lady with the right arm amputation, who's still rather shaken up—along to the home kitchen to the occupational therapist. She's going to try to show her how to make a cup of tea with her left hand, and you must stay with her for reassurance. OK?'

'OK, Staff, will do.'

Babs settled her uniform cap more firmly on her head and set off for the duty office, wondering why Sister had sent for her in the middle of a work list.

She arrived at the office, and found it full to bursting.

Guy was sitting on a corner of Sister's desk, and Sister was sitting, as usual, behind it, but in front of the desk, and spreading round the room, were the Newbrys, Mrs Pilbeam and the chaplain, as well as Colin and Liz.

The tension in the room was extraordinary. Babs was aware of it as soon as she entered, and a lot of people seemed to be talking at once. Babs's entrance silenced them, and only Sister's voice continued uninterrupted.

'Ah, Staff Nurse,' she said, quite unruffled by what was going on. 'I'm glad you can join us. I take it you are conversant with the problem that Colin and Liz have concerning their future.'

Babs's eyes met Guy's briefly, and she recalled their lunchtime discussion and his concern for their patients.

'I know that they want to get married,' she said cautiously.

There was a sort of muffled roar of anger from both the Newbry seniors and Mrs Pilbeam.

Mr Newbry said, 'But I'm sure you agree, Staff Nurse, that thinking of marriage is ridiculous in the circumstances.'

Babs wanted to say, What circumstances? but knew that she mustn't. It was her job to pour oil on the troubled waters, yet support her patients.

She attacked obliquely. 'I know that both Colin and Liz are young,' she said, giving them a smile. 'But they are both adults and are free to make their own decisions. I honestly think that it is up to them.'

'That's what I've been telling them till I'm sick,' said Colin. 'It's got nothing to do with anyone else what we decide.'

Babs felt a great well of compassion for all of those present. For the parents, who only wanted what was best for their children and were trying hard, but couldn't understand that love and passion could enter anybody's life if they were less than physically perfect. For Colin and Liz, who were just reacting normally to that wonderful ecstasy of feeling when two people destined for each other met.

Sister Crewe asked, 'Is there anything more, Staff, that you want to say?'

Babs felt uncomfortable at being asked so directly. She said hesitantly, 'Well, yes, there is. I think that everyone here should accept that they all want what is best for Colin and Liz, but I think that only Colin and Liz can know at this moment what they think is best for them. They want to get married — that's what they think is best — and perhaps they're right. Only time will tell, and that applies to any couple getting married, surely? Time is the deciding factor.'

She was acutely conscious of Guy's grave look of approval as she finished speaking, and wasn't surprised when he spoke with all his natural authority, endorsing her words.

Both sets of parents seemed surprised by what the nurse and doctor had said, and appeared for the moment to be lost for words.

It was Mrs Pilbeam who recovered first. Suddenly she reached out a hand and patted her daughter's arm, and said in a rather shaky voice, 'They're right, you know, love, and I've been very silly and over-protective. Just because my own marriage fell apart, it doesn't mean that yours will. In fact it might prove the opposite. Your dad and I were young and good-looking like you two, but we were strong and healthy; we didn't have any of the problems that you've got. Perhaps that was what was wrong with us: everything was too easy, and when there were problems we couldn't cope. You two will have more than your share of difficulties right from the start, and it'll make you both tougher. You've got my blessing and I'll do all that I can to help you get settled somewhere.'

Mrs Pilbeam's decision swayed the Newbrys. They couldn't go on opposing their son after the generous remarks that she had made about the prospects for the young couple. They weren't exactly enthusiastic about the idea of Colin's marriage, but they decided to make the best of it.

Sister Crewe brought the discussion to an end by suggesting that the two families and the chaplain make use of her office to plan wedding dates and so forth, while she, Babs and Guy went away to finish their work.

Outside the office, she thanked Guy for getting the protagonists together and forcing everyone to face facts. 'It might have misfired,' she said. 'But it didn't. You had the courage of your convictions.' She patted Babs's arm. 'And as I expected,' she said, 'you both spoke with great compassion and authority. Now away with you, Staff, and rescue the student. You can keep her with you till she goes off duty at five, and she can give you a hand with the multiple sclerosis lady, Mrs Morris; that is unless Dr Lloyd wants assistance with anyone?' She turned to Guy with a questioning look.

'No, thanks, Sister,' Guy said, giving her a nice

smile. 'I'm officially off duty as from now. And I want to speak to one of the physios on my way out.'

'Anything I should know about, Doctor? Is a patient involved?'

'No, it's personal,' he replied with a laugh.

'My apologies. I have no wish to pry,' said Sister a little stiffly.

'No apology needed, Sister, and you'd be welcome to pry.' He grinned cheekily. 'Actually it's my tennis partner; it's the finals at the end of the week, and I want to discuss tactics with her. We hope to beat Staff Nurse here and her partner Roger Mansfield hollow, as they look like being the opposition.'

'Your partner. . .that's Jane White, isn't it?'

Guy nodded.

'You know of course that she's leaving soon?' Sister asked, looking at both Guy and Babs.

They both nodded, and avoided each other's eyes.

'A great pity,' Sister continued. 'She's a splendid physiotherapist. You're going to miss her, Staff, aren't you?'

'Yes, I am,' replied Babs. 'She's a great colleague and a good friend.'

'Well, as long as you two don't go running off to foreign parts I don't mind what you do. I want this unit to go on to greater things. Now I must be off and so must you, Staff; don't be too long chatting up our clever registrar.' She gave them both a beaming smile, turned on her heel, and made off down the corridor.

'That canny old bird,' said Guy, with a quirky half-smile, 'knows that there's something going on between us, Babs, and, if she knows or guesses, so will the grapevine before long.'

'I don't think,' Babs said softly, suddenly conscious that they were alone in the deserted corridor, 'that Sister will gossip.'

She was standing with her back to the wall. Guy moved in front of her and placed the palms of his hands on the wall on either side of her at shoulder-level; his own broad shoulders, straining against the thin white cotton of his shirt, filled her view. She focused on the V of his open collar, where a fuzz of golden-brown hairs clustered just beneath his Adam's apple.

'Babs, look at me.' His voice was quiet but commanding; his warm breath fanned her face. Slowly she raised her eyes, following the sturdy column of his brown throat, the firm square line of his jaw, and the well marked mouth. The nostrils of his finely chiselled nose flared slightly, and above the bridge of his nose his blue eyes smouldered.

He didn't say anything immediately, just stood there looking down at her in the quiet, empty corridor. His eyes seemed to be taking in every detail of her face, slowly, as if he wanted to imprint each feature indelibly on his mind. She had never seen him look so absorbed, so tender. She caught her breath in a little gasp as he bent his head closer, and his eyes fastened on her mouth. He was going to kiss her. His lips touched hers, gently, fleetingly, and she closed her eyes and waited for his lips to close over hers with the passion and desire that he was holding back. She shuddered in anticipation, but the kiss didn't come. She opened her

eyes. His face was still close to her own, and he was
breathing hard, but he was shaking his head.

'Wrong time, wrong place yet again, my dear,' he
said softly, referring to their earlier meeting in the rose
garden.

He kissed her forehead, and pushed himself off the
wall, taking both her hands in his. There was still no
one about, but they could hear the murmur of voices
coming from the duty office. Guy squeezed her hands
gently. 'Wasn't it great,' he said, 'how things turned
out in there for Colin and Liz?'

'Wonderful.' She looked at him half fearfully, wondering if she could make him understand. 'Guy, those
doubts that I've had about us. . .'

'Seem ridiculous in the face of Colin's and Liz's faith
in each other.' She could tell from his tone that he
understood.

'Yes,' she breathed. 'I feel almost ashamed. We've
so much going for us, compared to them with their
problems. It seems cowardly not to take a chance.'

'A chance?'

She took her courage in both hands; it seemed the
right time, if not the place, to be totally honest. 'I love
you, Guy,' she said simply. 'I'm not sure whether you
love me half so much, since you haven't said, and I can
never quite be sure how you feel about me, but I love
you.'

Guy looked at her long and hard for a moment, then
lifted her hands to his lips and kissed her knuckles.

'That's to be going on with,' he said in a rather
detached sort of voice. 'After I've spoken to Jane, and
told her that you were the love that I hinted at, I'll tell

you how I feel about you, Babs. All you have to do is to wait until this evening, and trust me. See you on court.'

'Until this evening,' said Babs, as she watched him walk away down the corridor.

The rest of her duty period passed in a dream. She was walking on air. Guy had as good as said that he loved her. Nothing could go wrong now; they would find a way through any problems. Life was wonderful.

Still feeling on top of the world, she went off duty at six, and showered and changed ready to go to the tennis club and watch the first of the semifinals.

Jane and Guy were playing against a couple who were the greatest challenge to the four of them. Tomorrow she and Roger would play the other semi-finalists, with every likelihood of beating them.

And the day after tomorrow, mused Babs, as she walked slowly to the clubhouse through the burning evening sunshine, if the four of us come through the semis we'll be playing each other, and by the end of the week Jane will have left Princes. Hopefully, they would part good friends, and in her present euphoric mood she was sure that they would.

Nothing, she resolved as she approached the club-house, was going to spoil her happiness tonight; she was simply going to enjoy watching Guy move with athletic strength and elegance about the court.

The clubhouse and the terrace were full when she got there, with supporters of both pairs of players loudly voicing their reasons for backing their favourites.

Roger was waiting for her, nursing drinks and guarding chairs that he had bagged for them to take over to the main court, where the match was to be played.

'Babs, grab the drinks and I'll take the chairs,' he said as soon as he saw her. 'I want a ringside seat for this match.'

It was typical of Roger that he didn't mention their intimate conversation of the previous evening, or seem curious as to whether she had yet spoken to Guy; he was just keen to size up the opposition.

Babs shrugged mentally. His aloofness suited her. All she wanted to do was to sit and watch Guy, and dream about being alone with him later. She hugged her rising tide of excitement to herself.

They were in time to bag front-row positions, and when, a little later, the players came out from the changing-rooms Babs could see at once that all was well. Both Jane and Guy were wreathed in smiles, and looking fit and very dangerous.

Guy caught her eye, and gave her the thumbs up sign. A great wave of relief flooded over her. She returned his signal, and gave him a wide and loving smile.

'Well done,' she mouthed, 'and good luck.' He nodded and smiled in return, understanding that Babs was thinking of other things besides the match.

It was a splendid match, won in three sets by Jane and Guy. At the end of the match Gregory Hurst, senior physician, director of medicine, and also president of the tennis club, spoke a few words, reminding everyone that the second semifinal was to be played the next night, and the final the night after that. He

hoped that all those present would be around on those
occasions to lend support.

Everyone wanted to congratulate Jane and Guy, and
it was some minutes before the crowd round the court
thinned out and Babs and Roger were able to get near
them and add their own congratulations.

'It was a wonderful game,' said Babs, giving each of
them a kiss on the cheek.

'I'm glad that you thought so,' Guy said exuberantly
as she kissed him. He bent his head lower. 'We, or at
least I, was playing for you, Babs.'

The look in his blue eyes — a mixture of triumph and
sensuality — made her heart pump madly, and her
cheeks flush. 'Oh,' she stammered, lost for words. He
grinned wickedly, obviously aware of the effect he was
having on her.

It was fortunate that at that moment Jane suggested
that she and Babs walk back to the clubhouse together
while the two men go on ahead to get their drinks lined
up. Clearly she wanted to talk to Babs.

'I'm so glad,' she said, immediately the men were
out of earshot, 'that you and Guy are getting together.
Do you know, I think that I guessed how you felt about
each other almost from the start, though neither of you
gave anything away. It was just a gut feeling that I had.
At first I resented you, but I got over that when I
realised that I wasn't in love with him any more. But it
wasn't easy to dismiss years of adulation, and I refused
to give in straight away.'

'Well, I'm jolly glad that you did in the end,' said
Babs with a grin. 'Guy insisted that everything would
be all right, but I had my doubts.'

'He was right, of course, and eventually I realised that I couldn't go on forever being grateful to Guy for covering up for me.'

'What do you mean, "covering up"?'

'Hasn't he told you that I took an overdose some years ago?'

'No, he only said that there was something that he couldn't tell me about you.'

'Dear Guy,' said Jane. 'Always the gentleman.'

'What happened?'

'I decided that life wasn't worth living, took an overdose, and was found by Guy, who gave me an emetic, and walked me round for hours till the effects of the tablets wore off. I didn't have to go to hospital, and nobody else knew anything about it.'

Babs was quiet while Guy and Jane were away in the changing-rooms, mulling over what Jane had said to her. Roger looked at her, but didn't say anything, and she was grateful for his silence.

Guy, thought Babs, had behaved impeccably over everything. He wouldn't have abandoned Jane while she needed him, nor divulged her secret, though it would have been convenient to do so. He might be autocratic and demanding at times, but it was these very characteristics that made him a strong, loving and passionate man. All she needed now was the opportunity to tell him that she would go along with whatever plans he chose to make. She could rely on him utterly.

It was late before the clubhouse closed down for the night.

Guy asked Roger to see Jane to her car. 'Babs and

I,' he said, putting an arm round Babs's shoulder, 'have other plans, haven't we, love?'

Babs nodded. She guessed that, like her, though neither of them had shown their feelings, he had found the evening after the match had finished frustrating. They'd had to be polite and socialise, when all they really wanted to do was to be alone together.

'We're going for a drive,' he said softly as they walked away from the clubhouse.

It was a perfect late summer evening, with a young moon shedding a soft radiance over everything, but not strongly enough to dim any but the nearest stars. They sped along with the roof of the car down, and the lightest of breezes blowing cool and sweet on their faces.

Guy drove to the Heights, a series of small hillocks topping the undulating downs, across the valley from Princes. From here there was a panoramic view of the surrounding countryside.

For a few moments after Guy had switched off the engine they sat in silence. After the stress of the day and the frustrations of the evening, they both for a moment felt drained and unable to speak; they just sat and stared out at the silvery landscape. They could see the lights of Princes Park, high on the opposite hill, and the twinkling lights of the small county town of Princes Hollow below in the valley. On the Heights it was like being on another, distant world, remote, ethereal and blissfully quiet, except for the delicate, far-off fluting hoot of an owl.

Guy undid his seatbelt, and then Babs's. He smoothed her wind-ruffled hair back from her face with gentle fingers. 'Your hair looks silver-tawny tonight,' he said softly, 'on account of the moonlight.'

Babs ran her fingers over the short, silky stubble of his hair. 'Yours,' she whispered, 'is silver-silver. This is how it will look when you're mature and distinguished — silver-white instead of sun-bleached white.'

'Does that mean that you're going to be around to see me getting old and full of honourable years?' He ran his finger down her soft cheek and along the line of her jaw, and then tipped her head upwards so that she was looking straight into his eyes as he bent over her in the narrow confines of the car.

His eyes were just dark pools glinting with silver light, but she could see them still as the brilliant blue that they were. 'Yes,' she said breathlessly, feeling herself drowning in their blueness as she always did.

'No reservations?'

She shook her head. 'None.'

'Because of Colin and Liz and their faith?'

'Partly, but also because of Jane telling me how wonderful you'd been with her when she needed a friend most of all. I knew then that I could depend upon you utterly.'

'And you weren't sure before?'

'No, of you or myself.'

He put a finger to her lips, and shook his head. 'No more talking,' he said softly.

He kissed her nose, and her cheeks, and her forehead, and then his lips descended on her lips, and his tongue gently probed into her soft, willing mouth. His hands slipped down over her shoulders, his fingers found the buttons of her blouse, and then his hands were caressing her bare breasts until they were taut with longing.

Her hands explored his bare torso beneath his loose shirt. The hairs on his chest were soft, fine, long and silky, and she riffled through them with excited, sensitive fingers, tweaking them gently. His pectoral muscles were strong as whipcord, but smooth and rounded like his biceps. The whole of him was hard, fit, smooth and strong, and she longed to belong to him, utterly, completely.

He dropped one of his hands on to her bare thigh beneath her short skirt, and began to stroke her sensuously. Then he stopped, and slowly drew away from her, his lips parting from hers in a series of tiny brushing kisses. With careful fingers he rebuttoned her blouse.

'Now,' he said huskily, 'is not the time. I want to make love to you, and, my love, I will, but not here in the front seat of a car; that's too small for such goings-on.' He laughed, a warm, rich laugh. 'When we do make love, it must be perfect — the right time, the right place; no half-measures.'

It hurt that he had put her from him. She ached for him; she wanted him to go on touching her in all her most secret places, to excite her to the point of no return. But he had said no, and she knew that he meant it. She must try and match his self-control.

'Let's get out and walk and talk,' he said.

They walked in the moonlight, their arms entwined about each other, along the path that skirted the edge of the hill.

'It's like standing on the edge of the world,' said Guy. 'Just you and I alone in an empty universe.'

In spite of the sheer romance of the moment, standing there with a crescent moon above them, and the summer breeze rustling through the pine trees behind them, and her lover beside her, Babs couldn't suppress a giggle. Her practical common sense made her say, 'Alone in an empty universe if you ignore the lights in the houses on the hillside, and in the town, and, of course, in the hospital.'

They both stared across the valley to where the great rambling pile of Princes Park straddled the hill opposite. Even this late at night there were enough lights blazing for them to pick out various buildings.

'My darling,' said Guy with a theatrical sigh, 'you're definitely short on the romantic side. What am I going to do with you?'

'Be romantic enough for us both.'

'That won't be hard with you around, dear love. But I'm a practical man too. When we are married——'

'Is that a proposal?'

'Of course.' He went on almost as though she had not interrupted. 'We'll have to have somewhere to live, so we'll apply for one of the staff bungalows, and get married and live there. . .'

'Happily ever after, if I agree to marry you.' She gave him a dimpling smile, and he squeezed her waist hard.

'Well, not quite forever, not there. One day we'll be rich and live somewhere rather grand. . .'

'And you'll be knighted for your services to medicine. . .'

'And it will be Sir Guy and Lady Lloyd.'

They laughed happily together.

Then Guy was suddenly serious. 'Whatever way you look at it,' he said, looking down at her as he cradled her tenderly in his arms, 'we're going to have a long and happy life together, with no hang-ups. We'll talk our way through our problems; that's something that our work has taught us.'

'And never let the sun go down on our wrath, as my granny would say,' said Babs. She gave a gentle sigh. 'Do you know,' she added, 'I don't really mind if I stay just plain Mrs, as long as it's Mrs Lloyd.'

'Presumably that means that you've accepted my proposal of marriage, Miss Barbara Becker-Brown,' Guy said, smiling down at her. 'A very sensible decision.'

'Yes,' she said, 'isn't it?'

Guy kissed her in a very firm, decisive manner. 'I love you, Babs,' he said, 'with all my heart.'

'And I love you,' she said simply.

A little later, as the long, hot summer's day came to a close, they drove home in the moonlight to Princes Park, and their future there, together.

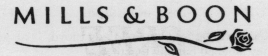

MILLS & BOON

LOVE ON CALL

The books for enjoyment this month are:

PICKING UP THE PIECES Caroline Anderson
IN THE HEAT OF THE SUN Jenny Ashe
LEGACY OF SHADOWS Marion Lennox
LONG HOT SUMMER Margaret O'Neill

♥ ♥ ♥ ♥ ♥

Treats in store!

Watch next month for the following absorbing stories:

NO MORE SECRETS Lilian Darcy
TILL SUMMER ENDS Hazel Fisher
TAKE A DEEP BREATH Margaret O'Neill
HEALING LOVE Meredith Webber

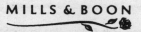

HEARTS OF FIRE

By Miranda Lee

✦ **HEARTS OF FIRE** by Miranda Lee is a totally compelling six-part saga set in Australia's glamorous but cut-throat world of gem dealing.

Discover the passion, scandal, sin and finally the hope that exist between two fabulously rich families. You'll be hooked from the very first page as Gemma Smith fights for the secret of the priceless **Heart of Fire** black opal and fights for love too...

Each novel features a gripping romance in itself. And **SEDUCTION AND SACRIFICE**, the first title in this exciting series, is due for publication in April but you can order your FREE copy, worth £2.50, NOW! To receive your FREE book simply complete the coupon below and return it to:

**MILLS & BOON READER SERVICE, FREEPOST,
P.O. BOX 236, CROYDON CR9 9EL. TEL: 081-684 2141**

NO STAMP NEEDED

Ms/Mrs/Miss/Mr: _____   HOF

Address _____

_____

_____   Postcode

mps MAILING PREFERENCE SERVICE